BLANCHE LANGDALE

THE OUTLAW'S BRIDE.

A Romance of Sherwood Forest.

BY THE AUTHOR OF "THE JEW AND THE FOUNDLING," "HEBREW MAIDEN," &c.

LONDON:

PUBLISHED BY E. LLOYD, AT THE OFFICE OF THE ILLUSTRATED EDITIONS
OF STANDARD WORKS, 12. SALISBURY SQUARE, FLEET STREET.

1847.

PREFACE.

THE reign of "Good Queen Bess" has ever been a favourite as well as a fruitful period with romancists, and it has also attained to great favour with that portion of the reading public which delights to wander in the flowery fields of fiction. The history of that era teems with incidents of a most interesting and attractive nature; and the character of the time was such as to ensure it a firm hold upon a vivid imagination.

Availing himself of these circumstances, so admirably combined and inviting to popularity, and believing that the path, however trodden by previous writers, might yet lead to exciting novelty, the Author ventured upon introducing the present production of his pen to a public which has always been liberal in their judgment of, and in granting their support to, those works which he hitherto has had the honour of laying before them.

The scene, too, in which the Romance of "Blanche Langdale" is laid is one familiar to us, time out of mind, and is hallowed with many a pleasant recollection. There it was that the bold Robin Hood and his merry men all held their rustic revels; and the shady glades of Sherwood Forest have ofttimes echoed to the swelling chorus of their manly voices. It is the scene, also, of the exploits of many a daring outlaw, who, clad in Lincoln green, and with his good yew bow, ranged the forest as he listed, unfearing and uncontrolled, killing a buck, or robbing a priest—and loved by the poor as much as he was dreaded by the rich.

That there was, in the materials he selected, a sufficiency from which to create a work of some interest, the Author is satisfied, from the great success "Blanche Langdale" has had; and it is no small gratification to him to find that the time and care he has bestowed upon it have not been thrown away, but that they have contributed in no inconsiderable degree to the entertainment of his readers.

For the past and present the Author returns his most sincere thanks and now has only to hope that the future may wear as bright an aspect.

LONDON,
January, 1847.

BLANCHE LANGDALE,

THE OUTLAW'S BRIDE.

𝔄 𝔕𝔬𝔪𝔞𝔫𝔠𝔢.

CHAPTER I.

> The moon pulls off her veil of light,
> That hides her face by day from sight;
> (Mysterious veil, of brightness made,
> That's both her lustre and her shade,)
> And in the lanthorn of the night,
> With shining horns hangs out her light.—HUDIBRAS.

BLACK, threatening clouds, the sure forerunner of a coming tempest, were ga
thering in the heavens, when two persons, the one young and the other middle-
aged, reached the borders of Sherwood Forest. Their way lay through the dark
mass of trees before them, but, being nearly strangers to the spot, neither of them

Seemed to know which of the numerous foot-paths would lead them to the place they were desirous of reaching ; and pausing to consider what had best be done, they turned an anxious gaze around them in the hope of discovering some cottage, where they might either inquire their way, or procure the services of some person to act as a guide. This hope, however, was doomed to be frustrated, and the younger then commenced a loud shouting, thinking to bring the assistance they were so much in need of ; but this scheme proved equally inefficacious, and the other, stopping him in the midst of his shouting, exclaimed :—

"I'll tell you what it is, Harry, you may bawl and call till this time to-morrow, for in a wild, out-of-the-way place like this, nobody will be likely to hear you."

"Why do you think so?" asked the other.

"You often call me a witless idiot," replied his companion, "but in this instance I can prove myself a man of more sense than yourself. You see what a storm we are likely to have before long, and yet ask why we are not likely to be heard, when any one may suppose that the peasant churls have sought the shelter of their own cottages, instead of strolling about to look after stray travellers."

"Peace, thou prating fool!" exclaimed Henry Neville, impatiently ; " and rather give me thine assistance in discovering some place of shelter, than thus aggravate our misfortunes by giving utterance to these senseless forebodings."

"What is it you want of me?" demanded the other, without appearing to be the least offended by the discourteous terms in which he had been addressed.

"In the first place, Master Nicodemus Dove, I would know how far we are from Holmwood Castle, the seat of my friend, Sir Richard Langdale?"

"How far?" reiterated the other ; "why, just far enough for us both to get tolerably well drenched with rain, if we are not fortunate enough to meet with a comfortable cottage and hospitable people to entertain us, between this place and the end of our journey."

"Pshaw! what am I to understand by all that?" exclaimed the younger man ; "I am in no humour for these idle jests, so tell me, in as few words as you can, how far it is from this place to Holmwood Castle."

"Well, then," replied Nicodemus, "though I cannot give very exact information, yet as near as I can guess—but mind, I won't answer for a furlong or two—the distance, I should say, is—"

"Ten miles, perhaps?"

"Nay! not quite so bad as that, either ; it may, however, be about the third of that distance—and, considering you are going to court fair Mistress Blanche, Sir Richard Langdale's daughter, it cannot be of any very great object if you should happen to get wet through, since the *warmth* of your passion for the maiden must be quite sufficient to prevent the possibility of your catching a *cold*."

"A witty speech, that, considering it came from the lips of an idiot!" exclaimed the other ; "but you spoke just now of Blanche Langdale, who, I believe, you have often seen?"

"I have!"

"And think you she is as fair as her sister Catherine?"

"Do you want my candid opinion?"

"Most certainly I do!"

"Then you must excuse me, Master Harry, if I answer 'No' to your question ; the girl is well enough, but since I have a sort of sneaking kindness for her sister Kate, I of course can see no one so fair as herself."

"Perhaps they are both equal in beauty?"

"Very likely they are," answered Nicodemus ; "but as I happen to be a bit of a poet, suppose I give you a description of them in verse—a few extemporaneous lines of my own, Master Harry :—

> My lovely Blanche is rather tall,
> Her sister rather shorter—"

"Peace!" exclaimed Henry Neville, impatiently.

"Nay," persisted the other, "I must finish the verse, in spite of your interruptions :—

> So list, my friend, and hear it all—
> *I* love the eldest daughter."

"A truce with thy folly, and answer me one question, so that I may under stand thee."

"Well, what is it you want to know ?"

"Is the report true that Blanche Langdale is sought in marriage by a mysterious outlaw, who infests the neighbourhood of her father's mansion ?"

"I have heard the rumour, and a good many people hereabouts think there's some truth in it."

"What says her father to it ?"

"That's more than I can tell you, though I rather think they've managed matters so well that he knows nothing of their having met. However, it must come to his ears by-and-by, and when the storm bursts, I shouldn't like to stand in the shoes of Blanche Langdale."

"Does her unknown lover venture to the house ?"

"He's often very near it," replied Nicodemus Dove ; "and, between ourselves, Harry, you stand a fair chance of losing your prize, unless you make up your mind to lose no time about making her your wife."

"You shall see that I am resolute, when a rival is in the way," exclaimed Neville ; "and if she proves to be worth the trouble, I'll find means to prevent her union with the villain you have been speaking to me about."

"Then you must take care to keep out of his reach."

"I shall rather endeavour to throw myself in his way," answered the young man ; "for I must see this rival of mine, who, they tell me, is not without a fair share of mettle."

"That will depend upon whether he chooses to throw himself in your way or not," observed Nicodemus.

"How so ?"

"Because they say he's for all the world like a ghost, and appears to people only when he's least expected."

"But he sometimes shows himself, I suppose ?"

"Yes, but only when he knows there's no danger of being taken hold of, though."

"What spot does he principally haunt ?" inquired Neville.

"There's no place in particular that I know of," answered the other; "but I've heard people say they have seen him three or four times at night-fall, wandering about on the banks of the river. Perhaps, like me, he's poetical, and goes forth to meditate in silence and solitude."

"I suppose, Master Dove, you have had your curiosity gratified by a sight of this extraordinary man ?"

"I should rather think I have too," answered the other; "and, what's more, I've tried to draw him into conversation."

"And there you of course failed ?"

"Why, I can say he has been very anxious to secure the pleasure of my acquaintance, but I've seen him, and that's more than a great many other people can say."

"Perhaps then, you can exactly describe to me what sort of a personage he is."

"I can," answered the would-be poet ; "his image is still in my eye, Master Harry, but you must excuse me if I attempt to describe his appearance in rhyme.

> He's a handsome, decent, good-looking wight
> As you'd see in a hundred men ;
> He's rather stout, and I think his height
> May be about five feet ten."

"A very accurate description indeed, Nicodemus," exclaimed the young man, hardly able to refrain from laughing aloud at the eccentricity of his companion. "So you have seen him, it seems, though he has not at present favoured you by entering into conversation?"

"That's no fault of mine, for I've tried it on pretty hard every time I've found myself within speaking distance."

"How did you contrive to introduce anything that might lead to a conversation?"

" By wishing him good night, to be sure."

" Which he of course took no notice of?"

"Not much, I must confess," replied Nicodemus Dove; " but one's obliged to be civil, you know, for they say he's so strong, that no other man is to be found who is able to bend his bow."

" How does he manage to support himself?"

" In the best way he can," replied the other; " he kills the deer in this forest at a pretty rate, for a week never passes that he doesn't shoot two or three of the fattest bucks in Sir Richard Langdale's domain."

"It is strange too," exclaimed the young man, "that Sir Richard allows him to commit these depredations without taking steps for having him punished."

"As for that," answered Nicodemus, "attempts enough have been made to take him, but they might as well do nothing, for the Outlaw goes armed with sword, dagger, and pistol, so that, there would be queerish work cut out for those that might attempt to take him."

"Would to Heaven I could meet with him!"exclaimed Henry Neville, "for then would we soon see whether he or I was to get the best of it."

" Are you serious in wanting to meet with him?" demanded his companion.

" So much in earnest am I," answered Neville, "that I should esteem it the most fortunate hour of my life if I could but find myself in his presence."

" If you mean it you may soon have your wish gratified," observed the other, for he is generally to be found at the cottage of Stephen Dagley, about this time in the evening."

"Where is the place you speak of?"

" About half-way between here and Holmwood Castle."

"But we are unable to find which is the right road that leads towards our place of destination."

" We'll have another try for it presently, though," exclaimed Nicodemus; "for we may find shelter from the evening storm in Dagley's cottage, and that's a prospect not to be forgotten on a night such as this is likely to turn out."

"At any rate, we shall get a roof to shelter us from the storm."

"Ay, from the wind, and the rain, and the thunder, and lightning perhaps;" observed Nicodemus Dove, "but I'm thinking if you should happen to meet the Outlaw, there'll be a storm of a worse kind before long."

"Think you, then, I fear to confront this man?".

" I don't know how you may feel about it," answered Nicodemus Dove, " but for my own part, I always had a mortal antipathy to be present at quarrels."

" You confess yourself a coward, then?"

" Not a bit of it," replied the other; " for I hold discretion to be the better part of valour. Besides, I may, myself, be dragged into the dilemma, and that's a thing that I'd rather avoid, if there's any way of doing it."

" Be that as it may," exclaimed Henry Neville, resolutely; " we will go there immediately."

. " Consider the danger, my dear fellow," cried the other, with alarm; " a quarre would be sure to take place, and then the only way to settle the difference would be at the sword's point."

" So much the better," returned Henry; " for, to speak the truth, Nicodemus, I long to measure weapons with the man who has achieved so much notoriety."

" Then wait some better opportunity."

" That may never occur."

" You can see him, I tell you, any evening, at the cottage of Stephen Dagley."

" If that's the case," asked Neville, " how is it that Sir Richard Langdale does not oblige this cottager to surrender this Outlaw into the hands of justice? "

" Do you really believe Stephen Dagley would give up the man that he has afforded shelter to? "

" Ay," replied Henry, " for, if called upon to do so, he must either obey, or receive the punishment due to one who gives shelter and concealment to a criminal."

" Pshaw! " exclaimed the other, " why, Stephen Dagley follows this poaching business himself, and it is not very likely that he'd give up his friend, when he knows to a certainty that it would be the means of sending him to the gallows. Besides, there is another reason why he don't want to turn the Outlaw out of his cottage."

" What is that, pray? "

" Why, the long and the short of it is, Stephen Dagley has got a pretty wench of a daughter, that they call Martha, and folks do say—but mind, I don't assert it for a fact—that her pretty face has drawn the Outlaw to the cottage of the old man."

" Impossible! "

" Why is it impossible? "

" Because your own words contradict yourself? " answered Henry Neville. " Did you not tell me just now that the Outlaw presumes to pay his addresses to Blanche Langdale? "

" To be sure I did," exclaimed Nicodemus, " and I still stick to the same story. Who knows but he pretends to court this Martha Dagley, that he may deceive Sir Richard for purposes of his own? However, there may be another reason, that I shall give in some original verses of my own composition :—

One girl's very well, but 'tis better, you know,
To have, when you can, *two* strings to your *beau ! ! !* "

" Prating fool! this buffoonery is unbearable," exclaimed Henry impatiently. " I would speak seriously upon an event that may turn out of the greatest consequence, and you treat the affair as if it was a mere joke."

" Ah! that's because you have no taste for poetry."

" So little taste have I for such as yours," exclaimed Neville, " that, unless you desist from annoying me with any more of it, I shall part from your company, and find my road to the castle the best way I can."

" Which you would be very unlikely to do, seeing that I, who know something of these parts, am completely bewildered."

" Then, for once, drop this folly, and act the more friendly part of being my guide. At all events, we must move forward, for see you not that the storm which has been so long gathering above us, is now about to burst forth with terrific violence? "

" Where am I to take you? "

" Lead me to the cottage of this Stephen Dagley," exclaimed the young man. " It may serve to shelter us for a while, and a lucky chance may throw in my path this mysterious outlaw, whom I have sworn to measure swords with on the first opportunity that offers itself."

" And if I do so, good Master Neville, will you promise not to fly into one of your confounded passions? "

" Lead on."

" Not till you have given the promise I ask for," exclaimed Nicodemus Dove. " I'm pretty certain you won't be able to govern your temper, and, if you should get into a quarrel with the Outlaw, the poor cottagers will be frightened out of their wits."

" I make no promises," answered Henry Neville; " for should I chance to meet my rival, no consideration shall withhold my arm from taking the vengeance I have sworn to accomplish."

" And why have you formed such a hatred for him? "

" That is a question that it is in vain for you to ask me," replied Henry Neville.

"Let it suffice that there is a feud between us, and that I never can rest satisfied till I have had the heart's blood of the man I am in search of."

"Revenge, Master Neville, is a bad feeling," exclaimed the other; "and if what you have said just now should ever come to the ears of Sir Richard Langdale or his daughter, you won't be thought any the better of for it."

"Perhaps not," answered the young man; "but at any rate I am determined, come what may, to have my revenge. However, you seem little disposed to guide me on my way, so the only thing that I can do in this extremity is to call loudly for assistance, and if anyone is within hearing, he shall have no reason to complain of the reward I will bestow upon him for acting the part of a guide to the cottage of this Stephen Dagley."

And again the impatient traveller called loudly; but, as on the former occasion, no answer was returned. The shout was however repeated three or four times, but still he was left in the same doubt and uncertainty as ever.

"It's all of no use, you see," exclaimed Nicodemus, "for, as I told you before, the people have all gone to their beds, so we must make up our minds to find the best shelter we can in the thickest part of the forest."

"You can do as you like about it," returned Henry Neville, "but I shall take the first path I come to, and trust to chance for reaching some place where I may get a lodging for the night."

"If you do that," exclaimed Nicodemus, "you'll find your mistake out, and be sorry for it when too late. However, a wilful man will have his own way; so, if you are determined to do as you have said, I shall beg leave to decline accompanying you any further on your way."

"Indeed! then you mean to leave me to my fate?"

"It's your own fault, and none of mine if I do," answered Nicodemus, "for I don't mind looking about in the open country for some place where we may find shelter, but hang me if I trust myself to the risk of groping my way through a dark, dreary forest like this."

"Do you know of any house where we are likely to meet with a night's shelter?"

"The only one I know of," replied Nicodemus Dove, "is the one I have told you of; and there I'm afraid to go lest you should find the outlaw, and then there would be a pretty kettle of fish between the pair of you."

"And what of that," demanded Henry Neville, "since you would not be called upon to take part with either side?"

"Very likely," replied the other; "but I should not be able to resist the temptation of giving you a helping hand, if it so happened that the other party was likely to get the best of it."

"If that's the case I've wronged you," exclaimed Neville; "and yet, after all, I cannot persuade myself to believe that you have so much regard for me as to bring you into a quarrel for the mere sake of helping me at a pinch."

"And, what's more, I don't wish to convince you of it," retorted Nicodemus Dove; "so be persuaded by me, and let us find a shelter anywhere else than in the cottage of Stephen Dagley."

"I shall not alter my intention if there is any way of carrying it into effect," exclaimed the other; and once more raising his voice to the highest pitch, he made so vociferous a shouting that anyone within a quarter of a mile could not have failed to hear him. The two then waited in silence for a few minutes, anxiously listening to hear if any response was given to their call for assistance. Once or twice they fancied they heard a faint cry in the distance; but as it came no nearer it was supposed to proceed from some of the birds that had been startled by the strange outcry, and the two friends were just beginning to despair of meeting with a guide, when footsteps were heard approaching, when a man of tall stature and rather ferocious aspect advanced quickly towards them.

"Who and what are you?" he demanded; "and why do you make such a shouting as if you wanted to alarm the whole neighbourhood, and rouse honest people from their beds?"

" We have lost our way," answered Henry Neville, " and felt no inclination to pass the night exposed to the fury of a tempest such as this is likely to be."

" You want a guide, then ?"

" Ay, if we can find an honest one."

" Well, *I* am honest," returned the man, " and you may consider my services as secured if you pay me for 'em by a handsome sum of money beforehand."

" You shall have three crowns, lawful money of our good Queen Bess," exclaimed Nicodemus, " so now move on towards the cottage of Stephen Dagley, if you know how to find it, and we'll follow you in all confidence."

" Answer for yourself alone in this case," cried Henry Neville; " you can trust yourself to this man if you think proper, but I shall remain where I am till I am satisfied that he belongs not to the band of marauders that I have heard infest this forest and its neighbourhood."

" If you take me for a robber you're mistaken," exclaimed the man, in a sulky tone.

" Perhaps so," answered Neville, " but you must convince me of my mistake by explaining why you are armed."

" Oh, that's easily done," returned the stranger ; " the truth is I am one of the keepers in the service of Sir Richard Langdale, and the reason of my being armed is, that I may be prepared against the attacks of the deer-stealers and poachers that prowl about this place o' nights."

" That's a fair explanation," interposed Nicodemus Dove, " and for my own part I really think we can't do better than put ourselves under this man's guidance."

" That is to say if I think proper to act as your guide after the suspicious hints that have been thrown out," exclaimed the man : " you had your doubts about me, and now, before we go any further, I should like to know who and what you both are ?"

" Why do you ask the question ?" demanded Henry Neville.

" Because I have a right to put it to all strangers that I meet with after nightfall," replied the man. " Sir Richard Langdale has given orders to take into custody an outlaw that has been prowling about these parts for some time past, and, for aught I know, one of you chaps may be the very person I'm looking for."

" Make yourself perfectly easy about that," exclaimed Henry Neville, " for I have the honour of being a friend of Sir Richard Langdale's, and was on my way to pay him a visit when night overtook us, and we have been brought to a standstill, uncertain which way to proceed."

" Are you a friend of my master as well as t'other one ?" asked the man in a tone that showed he was anything but satisfied with the answer he had already received.

" Friend !" exclaimed Nicodemus Dove, with offended dignity, " I'm something more than that, I flatter myself, for I shall have soon the honour to be son-in-law of your master, so you had better be civil, or I shall report your conduct and insist upon your instant dismissal from his service."

" What ! for doing my duty ?"

" If you know your duty, sirrah, you will act as our guide without further delay," exclaimed Henry Neville; " we have quite sufficiently explained who and what we are ; and now, in fulfilment of my friend's promise, here are three crowns, which shall be yours on condition that you conduct us without further delay to the cottage of Stephen Dagley."

" Stephen Dagley is suspected of being a poacher, so you can't want to be going there for any good purpose."

" Sirrah ! will you obey my orders or not ?" exclaimed Henry Neville, with increasing impatience. " I have heard the character of the man whose hospitality I seek, but this is no time for me to be particular about trifles."

" To be sure it aint," rejoined Nicodemus, " for the rain is already beginning to come down, and, after all, we shall scarcely reach the cottage before we are drenched to the skin."

"Follow me, then," said the man; "but remember, if any mischief should come of this visit to Stephen Dagley's, I'll not be answerable for what may happen."

As he said this he took a path that skirted the forest, and was closely followed by the two travellers, who, wrapped in their capacious riding-cloaks, seemed to bid defiance to the storm, which by this time had begun to realise some of the violence that had been anticipated. For nearly half-an-hour they pursued their way in silence, which was at length broken by Henry Neville, who inquired of their guide if he knew anything of the Outlaw, whom report spoke of as having sought a refuge within the purlieus of the forest.

"I know nothing more than what I have been told of him," replied the man.

"Have you ever seen him?"

"Yes, many times."

"Then you can tell me what sort of person he is?"

"Ay," answered the guide, "he is a fine, noble-looking fellow as ever I saw in my life. But I'd rather you'd find some other subject to talk about, for he's always wandering through the forest, and he wouldn't be best pleased if he should happen to overhear us talking of him."

"Nor is there much fear of his doing so just now," observed Henry, "for he would hardly be out on such a night as this; and if the report of my friend here is to be depended on, we are likely to find him snugly housed at the place where we are going to."

"If that should be the case," exclaimed the guide, "I'd advise you to appear as if you knew him not."

"And why so?"

"Because he's a sort of customer that you don't happen to meet with every day of your life," answered the other. "He has the strength of two men, and as for courage, I don't think the Queen has a braver fellow in the whole of her dominions."

"But he is an outlaw, and is one who sets at open defiance the laws of his country. He ought, long before this time, to have been safely secured in a prison."

"I don't know much about that," replied the guide, "but I believe there's very few hereabouts that would be inclined to try his strength against him."

"But many may be able to do what one is afraid to attempt," exclaimed Henry Neville. "Besides, a proclamation has been issued against him, and it is the duty of all loyal subjects to assist in apprehending him."

"Let those that think so be the first to come forward and take him," exclaimed the guide. "For my own part, I have too much regard for my own life to risk it against a man that I'm no match for."

"Then you neglect your duty to Sir Richard Langdale," answered the young man; "for I understand the Outlaw scruples not to kill the fattest bucks in your master's domain, and, as one of his keepers, you are bound to arrest the trespasser for pursuing his unlawful avocations."

"That is, if I should ever happen to catch him in the act of poaching," exclaimed the other. "I know my duty, sir, as well as you can tell it me, but I'll not raise my hand against this stranger merely because a cry has been raised that there may be no truth in after all."

"We shall see about that when Sir Richard Langdale hears the little dependance he can place upon his keeper," returned the young man. "I shall relate to him the conversation that has passed between us to-night, and—"

"In that case, sir, I shall take my leave without acting as your guide any longer. Yonder is the cottage of Stephen Dagley, where you may find the shelter you need."

And, pointing it out to them, the man turned upon his heel without deigning to accept the reward that was offered for his services.

CHAPTER II.

Draw, Benvolio, beat down their weapons:
Gentlemen, for shame, forbear this outrage.—SHAKSPERE.

WE must now precede the travellers, and introduce the reader to the cottage of Stephen Dagley, who, with his daughter, had for some time been anxiously waiting the return of those who were absent. At length, however, when the storm became most furious, Stephen rose from his seat, and, looking from the window to see if those they were looking for were approaching, returned once more to his chair, and expressed it as his opinion that his son and the Outlaw had sought a shelter from the storm somewhere else.

"They will not return to-night, my child," he said; "so see that all the fastenings are safe, and then to bed, for I have business to-morrow morning that will call me up betimes."

"Nay, dear father," she exclaimed, "shall we not wait a little longer for my brother and the outlaw stranger?"

"Ah! never fear for them, Martha," he replied; "they'll find shelter somewhere I'll warrant you, so that if the storm rages ever so fearfully you may rest assured they are not exposed to its rude buffetings. But tell me, daughter, why is it that you take so great an interest in this stranger, who, to say the best of him, is but a deer-stealer, and an outlaw to boot?"

"My dear father—"

"Nay, child, do not attempt to deny it—do not say that you love him not, for, though my hair is now turned somewhat gray with age, I do not forget the silent language of love that speaks from the eyes. Long and anxiously have I watched you both, for you have turned coldly from your former lover, Arnold Brockhurst, and this stranger usurps the place he once possessed in your heart."

"I know not how it is, dear father," cried the bashful girl, "yet I cannot but confess that you have looked more deeply into my heart than I had suspected."

"It is because I saw your growing attachment for our mysterious visitor, and at once foresaw all the evils that might arise from your over confidence in him."

"But even you yourself have expressed the greatest interest in the person we are speaking of."

"True, Martha," he replied, "I have offered him the shelter of my roof, and he has accepted it with the same frankness that it was offered. I had a warm hearth and a comfortable homestead, *he* was without a place to shelter him; and eternal curses light upon the man who would withhold his assistance from a fellow-creature who is languishing under the frowns of a cold-hearted world!"

"And then," continued Martha timidly, "he is in disposition so mild and gentle, in fact, so—so different from what one would expect from a man of his habits, that sometimes I cannot help thinking that he is a man of higher rank than he wishes us to believe."

"Ah! girl, that's just what I have thought about him sometimes myself," exclaimed Stephen Dagley. "But, be he rich or poor, great or small, he shall share the comforts of my cottage so long as he may need its shelter."

"Which I hope may not be very long," answered Martha, "for he hopes soon to receive the Queen's pardon, and, when that has been granted, we may expect to see him appear in a very different light to what he does at present."

"May be so; but you seem to forget that you will lose him as a lover as soon as fortune smiles more kindly on him."

"I have not lost sight of that," she replied; "but, whatever my own hopes may have been, I can resign them without a feeling of regret, so that I know he is happier than we have hitherto seen him."

"Can you then bear to behold him the husband of some female more favoured than yourself?"

No. 2.

"I can endure anything to see him happy," answered Martha. "His regard for me I believe is that of a brother for a beloved sister, and he may still continue to esteem me in that light even though he bestow his hand upon another."

"There is more danger in all this than you imagine," exclaimed Stephen Dagley. "Love is of too subtle a nature to be encouraged where the chances are all against you as in the present instance, and I would, therefore, fain prevail upon you, Martha, to show him how vain his proposals are, by bestowing more of your society upon Arnold Brockhurst."

Martha stood silent and uncertain what reply to make, and before she could give any answer a loud knocking was heard at the cottage door.

"Hark!" exclaimed her father, "some one knocks. Who can it be at this late hour of the night?"

"Shall I open it, dear father?"

"No," he exclaimed, peremptorily; "it's not you brother Martin, or he would have given the usual signal. Our midnight visitors may be robbers, perhaps, and these old arms of mine are not so well able to protect you as they used to be."

At that moment the voice of Nicodemus Dove was heard without, exclaiming,—

"What ho! within there! house! Stephen Dagley, for the love of charity open the door."

"Your voice is that of a stranger," answered Stephen, "and I will not open till I know your errand."

"That you shall know presently, knave," exclaimed Henry Neville, furiously. "Open, I say, without further parley, or, by hell! I will presently beat down the door, and take the shelter you would deny me."

"Once more I tell you I will not," replied the old man; "you have my answer, so now hence, for I decline all further parley with those who would threaten me with violence."

Scarcely had these words been uttered when, with a loud crash, the door was suddenly burst open, and Henry Neville, followed by his companion, rushed into the cottage. Terrified at the presence of strangers, and apprehensive of further violence, Martha threw herself into her father's arms for protection and support; nor was her appeal in vain, for Stephen Dagley, who had in the interval reached down a cutlas from over the chimney-piece, placed her on a chair, and then advanced towards them with a menacing gesture.

"Who and what are you," exclaimed the old man furiously, "that have dared to intrude yourselves in the cottage of Stephen Dagley against his will?"

"Who and what we are matters not at present," answered Henry Neville: "we asked for shelter, which was churlishly denied, and it was your own fault if the means we have taken to get in were somewhat of the roughest."

"Methinks you are a stranger in this part of the country," exclaimed Stephen, "or your wit would not have run in this wild fashion, for know, young stripling, that with a whistle on my fingers I can call as many stout lads to my assistance as will lay you upon the earth beneath my feet."

"Do you threaten me, villain?" exclaimed Henry Neville, drawing his sword partly from its sheath.

"I do," answered the cottager; "and will proceed to something more than threats unless you leave this place without further bidding to begone."

"Nay, then, listen to me," returned the other, resolutely; "if you do not instantly lay down your weapon, I will, with this rapier, strike your carrion carcase to the ground, as I would that of a dog!"

"Lay down my weapon?" exclaimed Stephen Dagley with scorn; "I'll lay it upon thy head first, and then, if thou hast courage enough to measure swords with me, this quarrel shall be settled by the death of one or both of us."

Unable to control his rage any longer, Stephen made a desperate assault upon younger and more vigorous antagonist, who, skilfully averting the weapon with his rapier, closed in, and threw the old man heavily upon the floor. In another instant he had drawn his poniard, and was about to plunge it into he heart of

Stephen Dagley, when Martha, with a loud scream, rushed forward and fell in supplicating attitude before the visitor.

"For mercy's sake, hold thy hand!" she exclaimed ; "indeed, indeed, my father thought you were robbers, or he would not have denied the shelter you asked."

"Say you so, my pretty damsel?" cried Neville, struck with the beauty and earnestness of the fair pleader. "He mistook us, did he? then for your sake I'll forego my revenge, and bestow upon him the mercy you have asked for."

As he said this he relaxed his grasp from the throat of Stephen Dagley, who rose from the ground somewhat exhausted by the struggle in which he had been engaged.

"You heard what your daughter said," continued Neville, "and I suppose you acknowledge her explanation to be a true version of the affair."

"I do," answered the old man ; "my daughter says truly, sir, for I knew not that you were peaceable travellers, or I should hardly have refused you admittance on such a stormy night as this. By the bye, though, your greeting has been rather a rough one, considering I had a right to close my doors against whom I pleased."

"And I had an equal right to insist upon your hospitality, when there was no other place within reach," exclaimed Henry Neville. "However, as both of us may have been somewhat too hasty, the best way is to say nothing more about it."

"Agreed ; and now that matters have taken so satisfactory a turn, you are welcome to my hospitality, and shall have such fare as my poor cottage affords."

"Why, now you speak more like a reasonable man," replied the other, "and, for your daughter's sake, I freely forgive the very indifferent reception you at first gave us. However, we want nothing of you, old man, except a shelter till the violence of this storm has passed over."

"I beg your pardon, there," exclaimed Nicodemus Dove ; "for since the old man has been civil enough to make the offer, we may as well partake of his fare, however humble it may be. Beshrew me, but the keen air has created in me an appetite that nothing is so likely to satisfy as a good substantial meal. Nay, I have just bethought me of a few original lines to soften that obdurate heart o yours :—

> Hunger, you know, is hard to bear,
>   They say it eats through walls of stone,
> So give us good substantial fare,
>   Good store of meat and little bone."

"Hold that fool's tongue of your's, Nicodemus, I command you," exclaimed the young man impatiently. "Let me hear no more of this vile doggrel, or your folly will bring down the chastisement it so justly merits."

Again a loud knocking was heard at the door, and the voice of some one without demanded admittance.

"Well, I declare!" exclaimed Nicodemus Dove ; "here's more visitors to fall foul of the cupboard."

"Some persons are at the door, sure enough," returned Henry. "Travellers like ourselves, perhaps, who have been overtaken by the tempest, and need the shelter we have ourselves been lucky enough to meet with."

"I hear the signal," whispered Martha to her father ; "it is my brother and his mysterious friend."

"It is," replied Stephen ; "so let them in, Martha, and leave the rest to chance."

"No, no, no," she replied ; "they must not come in while those persone are here, for I know their impetuous tempers will not brook the insolence we have ourselves received from these strangers."

"Hark ! they knock again," said her father ; "quick, girl, open the door—the rest we leave to chance and the courage of those who are now coming."

Unwillingly Martha obeyed his commands, and, the door being opened, Martin Dagley and the Outlaw entered the cottage. They both started on perceiving visitors, as if doubting whether to advance or not.

"Nay," exclaimed Henry Neville, as he perceived their hesitation ; "fear not to nter, for we are all friends here, and you have nothing to apprehend. By the by, gentlemen, how wears the night? has the storm abated any of its violence?"

" Ay," answered Martin, regarding the questioner with an inquisitive glance; " the tempest has nearly passed away."

" Is it near daylight yet?"

" Yes : the dawn is just breaking, and in a short time we may expect to have fair weather again."

" Well," exclaimed Nicodemus Dove, rubbing his hands gleefully, " that's th best thing I've heard anybody say for a long time. But tell me," he added, addressing himself to Martin, " you young wild man of the woods, is the bridge over the river passable for foot passengers?"

" No," he replied, " nor it won't be for some hours to come."

" Indeed! how is that?"

" Because it's buried in the flood, and no trace remains of where it is to be found."

" Then I'll tell you what it is, my young friend," said Nicodemus, addressing himself to Neville; " we must proceed by a more roundabout way; for somehow or another we must contrive to reach Holmwood Castle by breakfast-time."

" That will depend upon whether we can do so with safety."

" Safe or unsafe, I can't stay here much longer," exclaimed Nicodemus. " My bowels are already in a state of open rebellion, and the only way to appease them is to indulge in the substantial fare that Sir Richard Langdale always provides as a breakfast for his guests."

" For my own part, I am well content to remain where I am, my good friend," answered Henry Neville. " The storm is not yet quite over, so I shall take up my quarters with this bonny lass here, and you, if it suits your whim, may proceed the rest of the journey alone."

Whilst Neville was speaking this, Stephen Dagley had advanced, and, placing himself between his daughter and the young man, he exclaimed sternly—

" My girl does not detain you, sir. If you deem her a wanton that hawks about for strange gentry, I must be bold enough to tell you, your shot rambles wide of the mark. Come, Martha, my child, this is no place for you. Gentlemen, we bid ye farewell."

And, leading his daughter by the hand, he retired with her to another part of the cottage.

" Perhaps you will now favour us by leaving the place?" said Martin, addressing himself to the two travellers.

" I shall remain here or depart, as suits my own pleasure," answered Neville, sullenly.

" Humph! it shows not much courtesy, sir, for a sheltered man to rail thus against those to whom he has been indebted for whatever hospitality they had it in their power to bestow."

" Sheltered?—villain!—"

" Ay, sheltered! and yet no villain of thine," exclaimed Martin Dagley, " or I should serve a sorry lord."

" By my faith, scoundrel," retorted Henry Neville, laying his hand upon his sword, " if you had not called this maiden, sister, I would have slain you even upon the spot where you are now standing!"

" Now, I prithee, gentlemen," cried Nicodemus Dove, imploringly,—" nay, I do implore thee, not to endanger the Queen's peace in this manner, for if either of ye should be slain I shall be an unhappy man for ever afterwards."

Martin however took no notice of this, and, advancing towards Neville, he said contemptuously—

" Are you afraid of me?" he asked, " or do you wear too fine a doublet to trust yourself within the length of my sword?"

" Dog!" exclaimed the other, stung to the quick by these words, and instantly they were engaged in mortal combat. After a few passes, however, Martin was disarmed by the superior swordmanship of his antagonist, and, falling to the ground, he would have received the weapon of his opponent in his body had not the Outlaw, who had been anxiously watching them, rushed forward, and arrested the arm of Neville as it was about to inflict the deadly wound.

" Surely you would not slay him ?" he exclaimed: " he is conquered and at your mercy."

" I will show none to him nor to you either, if you do not instantly leave hold of my sword," cried Neville, after a vigorous but vain effort to release his weapon from the strong grasp of the Outlaw.

" You shall have it," answered the stranger, " but you will only retain possession so long as you abstain from further acts of violence against this young man."

" By what right, sir," demanded Neville, " do you presume to interfere in this quarrel ?"

" I am no party in the affair, sir, as you must yourself acknowledge," replied the Outlaw : " the quarrel was brought on entirely through your own insolence, and the punishment, if you had received any, would hear been richly merited."

" So you may think," exclaimed the other; " but I happen to know that he spoke words which no man of spirit would have without resentment."

" Be that as it may," answered the Outlaw, " I saw him powerless and at your mercy, and I could not stand quietly by to see a man murdered."

" Murdered !" retorted Henry Neville, indignantly; " were we not opposed together, point to point, as fair foes ?"

" True, but his skill in swordmanship was far inferior to your own."

" I believe the contrary," replied Neville, " and having conquered him in fair combat, I have a right, by the law of arms, to spare or slay him at my own discretion."

The Outlaw was silent for a few moments, and then, advancing close to Neville, he whispered in his ear—

" He was no match for a skilful swordsman like the well-practised soldier, Henry Neville. Ha! you start at hearing your own name uttered ; but, sir, I am in the possession of a yet greater secret. I know the treasonable plot in which you are engaged against our most gracious Queen Elizabeth, and—"

" Villain ! thou liest !" exclaimed Neville, unable to control his fury any longer.

" These are harsh words to use towards one who claims to be at least thy equal," answered the other, subduing the momentary anger which these words had given rise to. " I have known the time, young gentleman, when less provocation would have made my sword leap from its scabbard to punish the audacity of him who dared to utter them."

" Why not meet me now?" exclaimed Neville ; " if you want a weapon, here is the one I have taken from yonder churl ; but if you refuse my challenge, I shall henceforth look upon you as a coward who can bandy words with his tongue, though you dare not defend yourself with a sword."

" These taunts will not tempt me to break the resolution I have made," exclaimed the Outlaw ; " I am satisfied with having saved the life of this young man from your blind fury, and have no desire to mix myself further in a quarrel that did not commence with myself."

" It would have been far better if you had not mixed yourself in it at all," observed Neville.

" I should not have done so but that I saw the life of a fellow-creature was about to be sacrificed."

" Had he perished it would have been through his own insolence," replied Henry Neville.

" Perhaps so ; but it is one of the duties of a sworn knight, like yourself, to exercise some little forbearance towards those who happen to be betrayed into too much wrath."

" That is at our own discretion," answered Neville : " however, be that as it may, I have yet to learn by what authority it is that you presume to lecture me."

" The authority I derive from the right that every man claims to interfere when he sees the strong trampling upon the weak."

" Then I deny your right," exclaimed Neville, " and once more I challenge you to settle this dispute by fair duel. Take this sword, sir, and defend yourself."

During this altercation Nicodemus Dove had concealed himself beneath a table, but now he could no longer restrain himself, and, crawling from his hiding-place, he advanced between the two contending parties.

" Now, pray, dear, good gentlemen," he exclaimed, " do suffer yourselves to get a little cool before you go fighting about nobody knows what. Put up your swords I beg of you, and don't think any more of cutting each other's throats."

" Begone !" cried Neville in a voice of thunder.

" I will, if you'll go with me," answered the peace-maker.

" It's now quite daylight, good Master Neville, and if we don't make haste we shall hardly reach Holmwood Castle in time for breakfast."

" Wilt thou leave me, prating ideot ?"

" What shall I tell Sir Richard Langdale when he asks what has become of thee ?"

" Tell him what you like, but leave me, ere in my rage I turn my sword against thy worthless carcase."

" Nay, this is most unkind of you, Master Neville," exclaimed the other : " I am only anxious to save you from danger, and all I get for it is to be called scurvy names. However, if you will not listen to my entreaties, I hope you will at least remember that there is a young and pretty female in the house who will not think any the better of you for stirring up broils and disturbances in her father's house."

" There is no need to fear," interposed the Outlaw, " for I have, as you see, endured much without being provoked to fight, and he must find some more cutting insult before I can be tempted to turn the house of my friend into an arena for deadly and bloody strife."

" You hear what he says," exclaimed Nicodemus ; " he's determined not to fight, so imitate his good example for the sake of the poor girl that was the cause of the quarrel."

" Well, well," returned Neville, " for the regard I bear towards the maiden I will not pursue this matter any further at present. My sword I return to its scabbard, to be released only when a favourable opportunity offers itself for renewing this quarrel."

" Which I hope will never be the case," exclaimed Nicodemus Dove. " But see ! the sun is getting quite high up I declare, and if we waste any more time we shall be too late for our breakfast when we reach Holmwood Castle."

" I have told you already," said Martin Dagley, " that the bridge is covered with water, and if you go a roundabout way to the castle you will hardly reach it before night, for the waters are out all over the country."

" Oh Lord ! Oh Lord ! What's to be done now ?" exclaimed Nicodemus. Was ever anything so unfortunate as to be blocked out from the only place where we were likely to get a meal that's fit to be put before Christians ?"

" Cease these useless lamentations," cried Neville, " and let us make the best we can of our misfortune. Come, Master Dove, it's time that we speed on our way towards the Castle of Holmwood, for we have dangers to encounter, and if we take the necessary precautions to avoid them it will be some time before we reach the end of our journey."

" I begin to think very differently of this affair to what I did," exclaimed Nicodemus.

" Come, come, a truce to this folly ; we must be off without delay, so say if you are ready ?"

" Why, with all due submission to you, Master Neville," replied the other, " rther think I'm not exactly ready."

" Are you afraid then ?"

" I am ; and it's not much to be wondered at."

" What are you afraid of ?"

" Why, they say the bridge is lost in the flood ; and I can't quite make up my mind to admit that I feel the slightest inclination either to get a wet jerkin or a belly full of raw cold water when I've had nothing to eat for the last eight hours at the very least."

" This conduct of yours is most provoking, Master Dove," exclaimed the other. " I have business, as you know, of the most urgent importance to transact at the castle, yet you would now throw an impediment in my way, and perhaps ruin my prospects for ever."

" Oh, don't let me be any hindrance to you," answered Nicodemus : " go, my dear fellow, as soon as ever you please, only, under all the circumstances, let it be *alone.*

" Even as you will," answered the other ; "stay here as long as you please, but *I* will not delay my journey another minute, even though certain to perish by the flood."

Saying this, he turned away to leave the cottage, but paused as he passed the Outlaw, and whispered in his ear,—

" You seem to know me, and I have heard somewhat of you—you bear the name of an outlaw, but fear not that I am mean-spirited enough to betray you. Your defiance just now has given me too great cause to hate you, and if I have revenge it shall be with the aid of my own sword. Ere long, sirrah, you may rely on it, I will give you an opportunity of proving whether you have courage enough to meet me in single combat. Till that period arrives I bid you farewell."

Henry Neville darted from the cottage when he had uttered these words, leaving the Outlaw full of amazement at the open defiance that had been hurled at him. In a few moments, however, some new thought struck him, and, addressing himself to Martin Dagley, he exclaimed,—

" By Heaven ! the rashness of that young man will precipitate him into certain destruction ; for, impetuous as the current now is, it will be impossible for him to ford the river over, which he must pass ere he reaches the place of his destination."

" It will be his own fault if anything happens to him," returned the young man.

" True," answered the Outlaw, " but there will be much blame to me if I suffer him to perish without making an effort to save him. He must not—shall not die thus, even though he has declared himself my foe. Come, Martin, follow me, and we will pursue this rash man, and afford him our assistance should it be necessary. Follow me !"

Accompanied by Martin he rushed out, leaving Nicodemus alone in the cottage.

" Gone !" he exclaimed with alarm, " and I left here to find my way after them as I best can ! It will never do for me to stay here alone, so here goes to follow them as fast as my legs will carry me." And suiting the action to the word, he bolted out of the house and was in quick pursuit of those who had gone before him.

CHAPTER III.

Oh, bid me leap, rather than marry Paris,
From off the battlements of yonder tower;
Or chain me to some steepy mountain's top,
Where roaring bears and savage lions roam;
Or shut me nightly in a charnel-house,
O'er cover'd quite with dead men's rattling bones,
With recky shanks, and yellow chapless skulls;
Or bid me go into a new-made grave,
And hide me with a dead man in his shroud;
Things, that to hear them nam'd, have made me tremble;
And I will do it without fear or doubt,
To live an unstain'd wife to my sweet love.   SHAKSPERE.

WE must now proceed to Holmwood Castle, where the non-arrival of Henry Neville on the preceding evening had occasioned no little doubt and apprehension. Sir Richard Langdale expressed much alarm lest evil had befallen his intended son-in-law, and great was his chagrin when he saw that his fears were not participated in by the female members of his family. He, however, concealed his anger as well as he could; and having bade his daughters send out some of the servants in search of his expected guest, he himself left the castle to make inquires after him in the neighbourhood.

"And so, my dear sister," exclaimed Catherine Langdale as soon as they were left alone, "this ungallant lover of yours—this impassioned wooer—this Henry Neville, arrived not at the castle last night according to his promise?"

"His absence is certainly extraordinary, "answered Blanche, "but as for his being a lover of mine, I know not yet that he is so, for you, sister, have always shared as much of his attentions as I have."

"That may be," replied Catherine, "but never would I give my hand to one so base minded and heartless as this Henry Neville, and, if I do not greatly err in my judgment, Blanche, your heart is as indifferent towards him as my own."

"I cannot but admit the truth of what you say," answered her sister; "and it often grieves me when I reflect on the anger it will excite against me when my father learns that I am resolved to reject the lover of his choice."

"Our father knows not the perilous enterprise which Henry Neville has pledged himself to assist as far as lies in his power," exclaimed Catherine Langdale.

"True," answered her sister; "nor am I yet acquainted with that important secret, though you have often told me, Catherine, that at the first favourable opportunity you would acquaint me with the facts connected with his delinquencies."

"I have certainly made the promise," exclaimed Catherine, "and will now fulfil it in as few words as possible. You must know, then, that about three months since, whilst I was visiting at his father's, I accidentally discovered that this Henry Neville is engaged in a deeply-laid scheme, the object of which is to assassinate Queen Elizabeth.

"Oh!" cried Blanche, "is he so foul a traitor?"

"He is."

"Then why have you not before this time denounced him to those whose duty it is to inquire into the nature of a charge so grave and dangerous as this?"

"For a reason that you will presently admit is a sufficient one," replied Catherine, "and the discovery of which filled my heart with fear and anguish. The dreadful truth must however be at length revealed:—Our too confiding father is, I grieve to say, deeply implicated in the same treasonable plot, which has for its object the dethronement, if not the assassination, of our gracious queen."

"Oh, no, no, Catherine—it cannot—cannot be!" cried Blanche, burying her face in her hands, and giving way to all the anguish these words had occasioned.

"I was for a long time unwilling to believe that there was any truth in it," replied Catherine, "but from facts that have lately occurred I have now too convincing proof of the uth of what I had heard."

"He has been m d, then, by the artful misrepresentation of persons who would make him the ictim of their own crimes."

"That I believe, dear sister," exclaimed Catherine ; for from all I have been able to gather, I have every reason to believe that our too credulous father is but an instrument in the hands of this traitor and his equally wily accomplices."

"Still I believe there must be some mistake in this," exclaimed Blanche; "for, reckless as Henry Neville has ever proved himself to be, I cannot imagine any reason that he can have for seeking the life of so kind and beneficent a sovereign."

"His chief motive is to secure the aggrandizement of his own family," answered Catherine Langdale; "his father is nearly related to her who now so well governs the destinies of this nation ; he would exalt him to the throne, and then the full accomplishment of his designs would be achieved. His father has, however, refused to join in his rebellious designs, and even commanded him to quit the kingdom, as some punishment for the wickedness he has been guilty of."

"And did he quit the kingdom ?" asked Blanche.

"He did a few months since," replied her sister, "but returned almost immediately afterwards, bringing with him two other conspirators, whose daring natures render them dangerous to her against whom they are secretly leagued."

"Who are they ?" demanded Blanche eagerly.

"One of them is named Arnheim, a German soldier, and the other a crafty Jesuit priest, who the more willingly enters into the plot on account of the Queen's well-known leaning towards the Protestant religion."

"But you have not yet told me what part our father takes in this fearful business?" cried Blanche, anxiously.

"Alas!" sighed her sister, "I fear he is too deeply pledged to his associates to escape from the snares they have laid for him."

"Cannot we prevail upon him to abandon a design that must bring upon him ruin and infamy?"

"There is little chance of our doing so," answered Catherine, "for he is so deeply involved in the conspiracy that the withdrawal of his assistance at this juncture would lead to his inevitable destruction."

"How so?"

"Because Henry Neville is both revengeful and remorseless ; and he would, upon the least doubt being entertained, deliver him into the hands of justice."

"Which could not be done," exclaimed Blanche, "without bringing himself into trouble."

"You are mistaken there, my dear sister," answered Catherine; "for Neville would take care, before delivering up our father, to purchase his own safety as a reward for having revealed so dangerous a plot. But, hark! I hear footsteps : our father comes, and, perhaps, brings tidings of Neville's arrival."

Catherine had scarcely given utterance to these words when Sir Richard Langdale entered the room in which they were sitting.

"My children," he exclaimed, with more than his usual gaiety, "I have hastened hither to inform you that our long-expected guest has arrived."

"Is he in this house ?" demanded Catherine.

"He is," answered the baronet; "but having been obliged to swim across the swollen waters of the river, he has retired to his chamber to change his dripping garments. He will, however, be here in a few moments, and ——"

"His longer absence will be acceptable rather than otherwise to my sister," exclaimed Catherine.

"She knows her duty, and will not fail to perform it at the request of her father," returned Sir Richard. "However, I have some private business to confer with him upon, and must, therefore, request you to retire for the present."

"We obey you, father," answered Catherine; "yet, knowing something of the character of the man you have invited here, I cannot depart without entreating you to beware how you listen to the artful representations of a specious villain."

"Girl!" exclaimed Sir Richard, angrily, "is this the language in which you should speak of my friend, Henry Neville?"

"Henry Neville has earned for himself the character I have given him," answered the maiden. "He seeks to ensnare you in his web—would lure you to the path of destruction, and afterwards exult in the ruin he brings down upon his victim. Once more, then, dear father, I say, beware of Henry Neville."

"Hence, girls, hence!" exclaimed the baronet, scarcely able to control the anger that had been roused within him. "Leave me, I say, and, in future, learn to treat me with the deference due to a parent. Hence, I say!"

Grieved at the wrath he had manifested, Blanche and Catherine were about to quit the presence of their father, but ere they did so they returned, and, throwing themselves at his feet, implored his forgiveness ere they took their departure. For a few moments Sir Richard hesitated, as if unable to overcome his wrath, but at length, yielding to the better dictates of his nature, he folded them both in his arms, kissed their fair brows, and bade them depart with an assurance that he had pardoned them. But the words he had heard uttered were not to be easily obliterated from his memory; and as he paced rapidly up and down the apartment, he murmured to himself,—

"'Tis strange—passing strange—that they should exhibit this unwillingness to leave me with Henry Neville! Is it possible that they can guess the connexion that exists between us—the covenant by which we have both sworn to snatch the crown from the brows of her who now wears it? But no, no; it is impossible that they can have learnt the secret motives that have brought him hither. The fear that prompted such a thought is childish, for how can they have discovered a design so privately carried on, and which is known only to the few who are sworn never to reveal the plot, or to betray those who are leagued with them?"

The baronet was still occupied with these and similar thoughts when Henry Neville entered the room.

"Why, how is this, Sir Richard?" he exclaimed. "What has happened that I find you more moody and melancholy than when we just now parted? Has anything occurred to ruffle your temper, or give reason to suppose that our secret is not quite so safe as we believed it was?"

"No, no," answered the baronet, anxious to avoid an explanation of what had occurred; "we are so far safe; and if my brow was moody when you came in, it was only caused by a passing thought, which your presence has instantly put to flight."

"What!" exclaimed Neville; "you begin to feel some qualms of conscience about our notable conspiracy, I suppose?"

"No; my resolution remains unchanged."

"Why, that's well said," exclaimed the younger conspirator; "but, in faith, her Majesty had well-nigh been spared the danger that threatens her, since I, its chief agent and instigator, had nearly lost my life in the flood caused by the over-swollen waters of your river. But to our business, Sir Richard; for I would know if you are prepared to strike, without any further delay, the blow we have so long meditated."

"I am," answered Sir Richard Langdale; "but ere we commit ourselves too far, I would know what chance we have of bringing this affair to a successful termination."

"Everything is as favourable to our designs as can well be," replied the other. "Father Francis and Arnheim are ready to co-operate with us at a moment's notice, and, according to the arrangements I made with them, they are to arrive in this neighbourhood in the course of to-day."

"So far our scheme proceeds well," exclaimed Sir Richard; "but there is one thing that I fear goes sadly against us."

"What is it?"

"That your noble father, Lord Elrington, still obstinately refuses to join with us."

"He does so," answered Neville, "and his refusal is the more to be regretted, since it is not the pretence of moderation that would have kept Elizabeth on the throne till this time, had my father given us his powerful support. We must, however, do without him ; and I would now learn, Sir Richard, the amount of assistance you are prepared to bring in aid of the cause in which we are engaged ?"

"I have not been idle," replied the baronet ; "and, knowing as I do the devoted attachment of my vassels, I can promise the faithful assistance of a few score men, who may be relied on when the moment of action arrives."

"Will they be ready at our first summons ?"

"They will," answered Sir Richard ; "but in what way do you propose that we shall first proceed ?"

"Caution must be our first care," exclaimed Henry Neville. "We must give our cunning confederate, Cardinal Morton, full information of the exact situation in which our affairs now are."

"Methinks that should have been done before."

"It has been done," answered Neville, "for I have already sent a messenger to him with a letter, describing what has been done, and what we propose doing next. In a short time we shall receive his answer, and by that we shall be guided in the steps that are to follow."

"How long will it be before we hear from him ?"

"That will depend upon what obstructions our messenger may meet with on the road," answered Henry Neville. "In the mean time, however, we must have more money, men, and arms, or the good cause will be lost ere our plot is thoroughly ripened."

"Never," exclaimed the baronet ; "never shall it be lost while I have a coin left in my power, or strength in this right arm. Either Queen Elizabeth must descend from her present exalted station, or I will be content to lay down my own life in a cause that I believe to be a righteous one."

"Your resolution augurs well for the future," exclaimed Henry Neville, "and I now begin to believe that you are as earnest in this cause as I am myself. We have never yet acknowledged the right of Elizabeth to the throne of these dominions, and I can see no reason why we should endure the sway of one opposed to us in religion and everything else that we hold dear to us as life itself."

"Yet there are some," observed Sir Richard, "who hesitate not to say that in her heart she is a true Catholic."

"Believe not those who say so," exclaimed the other, "for the persecution we have endured is of itself enough to prove that she is a merciless and unrelenting enemy. She is opposed to us in religion, Sir Richard, and, like a tyrant as she is, would hunt us from the face of the earth for daring to entertain an opinion different from her own."

"But the tables, if I mistake not, will soon be turned."

"Ay," answered Henry Neville, with malicious satisfaction ; "but the hour of our triumph at length draws nigh ; the plot that has cost us so many days and nights of anxiety is nearly ready ; and then the haughty Elizabeth may tremble, for the just vengeance of those who have been persecuted for conscience sake will at length overtake her."

"What mean these words ?" cried Sir Richard Langdale, startled by the vehemence of his young friend. "Surely, Neville, you would not murder a helpless woman ?"

"Murder her !" retorted the other, bitterly. "No, no, I would not murder her with my own hand, Sir Richard ; but, if I saw the dagger gleaming above her head and the arm of the avenger about to strike the fatal blow, I would not cry 'Hold' though even that one word might save her."

"And yet, I thought our design was either to imprison the queen, or send her to pass the remainder of her days abroad ?"

"Such was the plan once proposed," answered Henry Neville, "but never can we consider ourselves safe whilst the deposed sovereign exists. From a prison she might escape—in exile she would still be a dangerous foe, and nothing but her death can give us security."

"Yet the alternative is a dreadful one."

"It is," returned Neville ; "but, as men whose lives depend upon a desperate act, we must not in the eleventh hour shrink from it. Duty, honour, patriotism, all demand our unshrinking and firm support, now that we have so far succeeded in perfecting our plot. But, hark ! I hear footsteps coming this way —we are interrupted, Sir Richard, and if my ears deceive me not the voice is that of the young woodman, Martin Dagley."

As he said this, the person he had named entered the room, and, bowing to the two gentlemen, he stood as if waiting to hear if there were any commands for him."

"Well, Martin," exclaimed the baronet, "what brings you to the castle this morning? Have you been again found poaching on my domains?"

"No, Sir Richard," answered the other ; "I have come on an errand to Master Henry Neville."

"A message to me?" exclaimed the young man."

"Ay," replied Martin, "and one that I believe concerns you rather nearly."

"In that case," said Sir Richard Langdale, "as Martin seems to have a secret to communicate, I will leave you with him for the present. I have a few letters to write in furtherance of the project we have in view, and will return again as soon as I have finished them."

Upon this he left the room, and Henry Neville, addressing himself to the messsenger, exclaimed,—

"Now, sirrah, be brief, and deliver the message you are charged with—quick, man, for I have little time to spare."

"Well then," answered Martin Dagley, "I have come to tell you that two mysterious-looking men have arrived at my father's cottage, where I left them when I came away."

"How do you know that they are acquaintances of mine?"

"Because they made a great many inquiries about one Henry Neville; and learning that you had come on to Holmwood Castle, I was immediately despatched with a message, desiring you to meet them."

"Humph! Do you happen to know the names of the persons you are speaking of?"

"Lord bless you, not I !" answered the young man.

"They did not tell you who they are then?"

"No," answered Martin, "and they seemed to take devilish good care not to be known. For all that, however, I could understand quite enough to convince me that one is a Roman Catholic priest in disguise, and the other by his lingo seems to be a German or some other foreigner."

"So, so!" muttered Henry to himself; " 'tis then as I suspected—the Jesui and Arnheim are close upon my heels, and our plot proceeds most favourably Then, addressing himself to the messinger, he continued,—" You have done we, my friend, in bringing me this information so early, so here is money to repay yu for the trouble you have taken."

"What am I to do next?" asked Martin.

"Why, return without delay to those who sent you, and say that I will ait upon them as soon as possible."

"They wished you to return with me."

"Tell them I cannot do that without acting discourteously to those whom it is my interest to keep in favour with," answered Henry Neville. " I will b pay my respects to the two daughters of Sir Richard Langdale, and within a hour from this time will set forth to meet these strangers at your father's cottag

"Why, as to the young ladies, sir," exclaimed Martin Dagley, " I belie you may spare yourself the trouble of seeking them, for while passing on my way hither I met them both taking their usual walk towards the forest."

"The forest !"

"Ay, sir; a day scarcely passes that I don't meet them going in that direction."

"Know you what they go there for ?" exclaimed Henry Neville. "'Tis a lonely place for females to walk to, and I should have thought they would have been afraid of meeting the Outlaw, who report says has for some time past made that wild spot his place of resort."

"Afraid !"

"Yes—for they cannot go there without danger."

"Why, Lord love you, sir ! I believe it's for the very purpose of meeting him that they go there so often."

"What mean you, sirrah?" demanded Neville angrily.

"Why, to speak the plain truth, sir," answered Martin Dagley, "I have heard it said that the baronet's eldest daughter, Miss Blanche, and the Outlaw you are speaking about, are over head and ears in love with each other. But don't frown so angrily at me, sir, for I know nothing more than what folks say ; though, to be sure, I've often seen them talking together in private when they have thought no one was near to watch their billing and cooing."

"May my eternal curses cling to this officious Outlaw !" exclaimed Henry Neville, unable to restrain his passion any longer. But he shall not again escape me, for my arm shall punish his presumption, and, should we chance to meet this day, the fate of one or both of us shall be sealed."

Excited to the utmost fury he rushed out of the room, and as he did so Martin Dagley burst into a loud laugh of derision.

"Ha! ha! ha!" he shouted ;—"*he* talk of measuring swords with the Outlaw ! Why, as well might he attempt to overturn the Castle Hill of Nottingham as to get the better of that mysterious man."

He was thus amusing himself with the notion of a meeting between the two parties when Nicodemus Dove, drenched with water and covered with mud, entered the room. In fact, the transformation was so complete that for a moment or two he knew not who it was that had so unexpectedly appeared before him.

"Hilloa !" he exclaimed, "what strange-looking animal have we got here ? By my faith," he added, upon recognising him, "'tis no less a personage than Nicodemus Dove, and a very pretty pickle he seems to have got into since I saw him last."

"Ah ! Martin, my dear boy," exclaimed the other, "I'm glad to meet with a human being once more, for here have I been wandering all over the house, and the devil a soul have I been able to meet with to give me a change of clothes."

"What's the matter with you ?" demanded Martin, scarcely able to refrain from laughing aloud.

"What's the matter with me ?" demanded Nicodemus. "Don't you see what a miserable plight I'm in ?"

"I do see that you are both wet and dirty," answered the other ; "but you have got to tell me how you got into such a plight."

"Don't stand laughing at me you, scoundrel," exclaimed Dove, "and I'll presently tell you all about it. First of all, then, you must know that after leaving your house I saw that mad-brained foolish fellow Henry Neville dash into the deepest and broadest part of the river, and swim across. But I, more prudently, took a narrow part, where there was less depth of water, and, as it happened, a considerably greater quantity of mud. There, having got *half way over*, I stuck in the *middle*, where I might have remained till doomsday had I not been assisted out of the dilemma by that stranger we met with at your father's cottage. However, to proceed poetically :—

> He jump'd right in, and didn't care,
> But seiz'd me by my flowing hair.
> Then, holding out to me his hand,
> He dragg'd me safely on to land."

"That was civil of him at any rate," exclaimed Martin Dagley; "and being on shore, pray what did he do next?"

"What did he do?" returned the other; "why, I suppose he vanished in smoke or something of that kind; for, on turning round to thank him for what he had done, I found that I was standing there all alone by myself."

"Ah! that's just like him," exclaimed Martin; "for whenever he does a good-natured action, he always cuts away before anybody can have time to thank him. But how is it that you have not changed your wet clothes for dry ones before this time?"

"Because I've not been able to meet with any one since I came here, except yourself," replied Nicodemus Dove. "When the chap left me so mysteriously I made the best of my way to the castle, expecting as a matter of course to meet with a *warm* reception after the *cold* ducking I'd had."

"Well, and you have not been disappointed I hope?"

"Disappointed!" echoed the other; "why, I've met with nothing but disappointment ever since I came to the place. On asking for Sir Richard Langdale his grinning scroundrels of servants told me that he was busily engaged, and could not be disturbed on any account. I then asked to be introduced to the young ladies, in hope that my uncomfortable situation would obtain for me their pity and a dry suit of clothes; but there I was doomed to be disappointed again, for they are both gone out to take a walk, and nobody knows when they are likely to return home. I next heard that my travelling companion, Henry Neville, was in this apartment, but, as I was coming here in search of him, I met my gentleman full tilt, and, instead of answering my question, he bounded past me as if I were nothing or nobody!"

"Well then," replied Martin, "if you can't find any other friends, I'll be one to you. So follow me, and I'll take you to the steward's room, and you shall have not only a change of apparel, but something inside you to keep out the cold."

"Say you so, my good fellow?" exclaimed Nicodemus with delight; "then, egad! you're the best friend I've met with since my arrival at the castle. So to speak in the language of the Muses,—

> Proceed, my friend, and lead me where
> I soon may find repose;
> My hunger craves substantial fare,
> My body, drier clothes."

"Ha, ha, ha!" laughed Martin Dagley, "is that the way the Muses, as you call 'em, speak?"

"It is," he replied, "and in my opinion their language is a very choice one. I have been gifted by 'em, Martin, and never do I speak so well as under their inspiration. To be sure, my friend Henry Neville never likes to hear my poetry; but it's all owing to his want of taste, and I can always revenge myself upon him by extemporizing a few lines when I know he's not in a humour to hear 'em."

"You must mind how you put him out of humour though," exclaimed the other; for he seems to be a peppery tempered chap, and as he wears a sword by his side there's no knowing what use he might make of it."

"Tush, man!" returned Nicodemus; "don't I wear a sword by my side as well as Henry Neville, and do you think I'm not able to make use of it as well as he can?"

"I don't know how that may be," replied Martin Dagley, "but I think you'd have very little chance against the practised skill of a soldier if you came to close quarters with him."

"There's no chance of my ever doing so, my good friend," cried the other, "for I can always keep my temper when he loses his ; and as for what he says against my poetry, I can pocket the affront and pity the poor deluded creature that has no taste for the sublimities of genius. But I am cold and wet, friend Martin, so lead me forthwith to the presence of the steward you were speaking of just now."

Laughing heartily at the eccentricities of the self-dubbed poet, Martin Dagley conducted him from the room without further delay.

CHAPTER IV.

Mortal of ambitious mind,
Keep thy wishes aye confin'd ;
Let them not too freely soar,
Lest they fall to rise no more.—JOHN SAUNDERS.

AFTER the departure of their messenger to Henry Neville, the two conspirators sat themselves down in a room by themselves to concert such means as were best calculated to bring their views to a successful termination. They, however, soon found that very little progress was to be made without the presence of him who was their guide and adviser in every situation of difficulty ; and as time passed away without bringing him whom they expected, they grew more and more impatient lest all the trouble they had taken should be thrown away. The German, however, was the more irritable of the two, and having waited as long as he thought they ought to do he burst forth in no very measured terms against what he termed the indifference or carelessness of their colleague.

"What ails you now, Arnheim?" at length demanded the Jesuit, who had listened to him for some time without appearing to notice anything that had been said : "you seem to have worked yourself into an ill humour, and yet for my own part I see no reason to grumble till we know whether there may not be sufficient cause for the long delay of our friend."

"Der teuful !" exclaimed Arnheim ; "what for makes you so cool, when we neither of us know what danger we may be in if your friend means to play us a scurvy trick?"

"Scurvy trick !" answered the Jesuit; "and pray what interest can he have in doing anything of the kind ?"

"I don't know anything about that," answered Arnheim ; "but he's longer gone than there was any occasion for, and it begins to look queer that he comes not back according to his promise, when he knows a couple of jontlemens are waiting for him.

"Pshaw !" exclaimed the other, "don't let that trouble you, for our young friend will be here before long, I dare say. Henry Neville is not to be suspected of playing us false, and is too ardent in the cause in which we have embarked to forsake us now that he knows our plot is so nearly ripe for execution, and especially as he has seen quite enough to prove that we are pretty certain of being on the winning side."

"Verdammlich ! "growled the German ; "dis country, I believe, is going hell-ward like de devilish lurch of a ship dat is sinking in fifty fathom of water."

"What have you got to grumble about, I should like to know ?" demanded the Jesuit. "If we succeed in the business we have undertaken, there'll be a large sum of money find its way into your pocket ; and if we fail, I can't see much reason that you will have to find fault, seeing that means have been already taken to secure your escape before the people of this country can lay hold of you."

"How do I know that I'm safe?" exclaimed Arnheim. "These people say that I shall get clear off if there should be a discovery; but if once they should happen to lay their cursed paws upon me, the game would all be up, and nothing that I could say would get me out of their clutches."

"Perhaps not, but there's no occasion, that I can see, for your getting into their clutches."

"That's because you have a better opinion than I have of this young fellow that we suffer ourselves to follow as if he was something better than ourselves. I myself thought at first that he was of the right sort; but when we came close to the pinch I began to see that he would make a cat's paw of us, and we may go to the devil for aught he cares when once his own purpose has been served."

"You think him then both a coward and a villain?"

"He may be both for aught I know," replied Arnheim; "but even if he is neither I should rather keep a sharp eye upon him than place too much dependance where we may afterwards be betrayed."

"Would you dare say as much in the presence of the person we are speaking about?"

"Perhaps not," replied Arnheim; "because I happen to know that he is a hot-headed fellow, and I've no wish to have a brace of bullets through my brain for speaking my mind a little too plainly."

"You seem to have formed rather an extraordinary notion of the person you have undertaken to serve," exclaimed the Jesuit, eying his companion with distrust.

"I don't think differently of him now to what I have always done," answered the other. "Poverty made me glad to accept the terms he offered for my assistance in this business, but it don't follow that I'm to be satisfied with him when I see reason to believe he means to play us false."

"You can see no reason to think anything of the kind," cried Father Francis. "The plot we are engaged in is entirely under his management and control; he has so far kept faith with us, and we have no reason to believe that he will prove unfaithful to the cause, or to those who are engaged with him."

"Then why does he keep away from us when he knows how anxious we are for his return?"

"That is a question that you must put to himself, for I do not pretend to know anything more of his doings than he thinks proper to tell me without being pressed to do so."

"Then I must ask somebody else that may know more about him than you pretend to do," exclaimed the German; and, raising his voice, he called upon Dame Dagley to make her appearance in the room.

"Well, sir," responded the old woman, as she presented herself before them; "what is it you want with me? I am here to do your bidding."

"Where is this young gentleman, we bade you send for?" asked the German, impatiently.

"Marry, sir, how should I know where he is?" answered the old woman; "I have sent my son Martin to the castle for him, and it can't be very long, I should think, before he returns."

"Did you tell him to bring the gentleman with him?"

"I told him to do so if he could," replied Dame Dagley; "but you've got a wrong sort of customer to deal with if you think young Henry Neville is to be brought where you like at the beck of your finger. He boasts of being his own master, and won't stir for any one, unless he happens to be in the humour for it."

"He must stir for us, then," exclaimed Arnheim; "for I happen to have a spirit as great as his own, and, unless he falls a little into my notions, I may, perhaps, take into my head to leave England without the ceremony of bidding him good-bye."

"You had better not do that, if you'd keep friends with him," returned the old woman. "What your business with him may be I neither know nor care; but he's a dangerous man to trifle with, and so you'll find to your cost, if you do any-thing to offend him."

"I thought he was a stranger in these parts?" observed the Jesuit.

"Not so much of a stranger as you may fancy," exclaimed Dame Dagley. "He has been at the castle a good deal within the last few months ; and, if people report truly about him, he has some dark thoughts in his head that may bring him into trouble, if he don't mind what he's about."

"Have you heard any rumours about the business that brings him into these parts ?" demanded the Jesuit, eagerly.

"There's so many different reports, that I don't know which to believe," returned the old woman. "However, it's pretty certain there's mischief brewing somewhere, though I can't think, as some people do, that Sir Richard Langdale is concerned with him in a plot against her most gracious Majesty."

Father Francis was about to protest against such an absurd notion, but, before he could make his intended reply, a knock was heard at the cottage door.

No. 4.

"He is here," exclaimed the Jesuit. "I know his signal, Dame Dagley, so open the door and admit him without delay, for he comes on weighty business, and there is not much time for us to confer about it. Quick, I say, and let him into the cottage."

The old woman promptly obeyed his command, and, the door having been opened, Henry Neville entered, and warmly greeted the two persons who had been waiting for him.

"Welcome, welcome, my friends," he exclaimed; "I have longed to see you both, and this meeting inspires my heart with fresh confidence that our cause is going on prosperously."

"There is nothing to fear so long as we remain true among ourselves," answered Father Francis.

"Wohl!" exclaimed the German; "it's all very well to make sure of success, but is everything put in a right train?"

"Nothing, I believe, has been neglected," replied Henry Neville. "The corn is now ready for the harvest, and an abundant one it is likely to prove, if we take proper means to husband it well."

"Ay," observed the Jesuit, "if there are reapers enough, and they can find sickles to do the work. But is it safe, think ye, friends, to talk of this matter in the presence of a woman who is a stranger to us all?"

Dame Dagley, who had seated herself behind them, now rose, and approaching them, said, haughtily,—

"Shall I quit the room, sirs, whilst you finish this business of yours? You may, perchance, think that I am so dull of wit as not to understand what you have met here to talk about."

"The devil!" muttered Arnheim; "what does the old hag mean by these words?"

"I mean," she replied, in a significant tone, "much as you may doubt my knowledge, that ye are three noble gentlemen, who have a *good cause* in hand, that ye are anxious to bring to a successful conclusion. Heaven prosper it! say I;—and I know one that will not fail to help you with something more than fair words and good wishes."

"Is the woman mad?" exclaimed the German, alarmed at hearing her speak so freely upon a subject that required the utmost secresy and caution.

"What mean you, my good dame?" demanded Father Francis, with as much alarm as that which was felt by the German.

"I will tell you what I mean presently," she replied, opening the door and looking cautiously out; then, having satisfied herself, she returned to them once more. "We are alone," she continued, in a whisper, "and ye may now speak your minds freely if you are not afraid of me."

"Nay," exclaimed Henry Neville, "let it be thy task to speak first, dame;—you spoke just now as if you guessed who we are, and what motives we have in view;—what dost thou take us for, Dame Dagley?"

"By my faith, I know you well enough, Master Neville," she replied. "Last night, when you sought shelter here with your fellow-traveller, Nicodemus Dove, I was a-bed in the loft overhead, and, on hearing the affray you had with our wilful folks, I rose up and peeped at ye through a chink in the flooring."

"Well," exclaimed Henry Neville, "and what would you have us understand by all this?"

"That ye must mind lest others discover ye as I have done," she replied. "I honour the cause in which ye have engaged yourselves, but my husband and my children are not to be trusted, neither Stephen nor Martin, though the last is none so bad when he is called upon to take part in anything that he can enter into with heart and soul."

"We will be careful of them," exclaimed Henry Neville; "and do you take heed, woman, lest a word or a hint should betray the affair in which we are engaged. By-the-by, Dame Dagley, I would ask of you who that other person was that I met here last night. I have heard that he is an outlaw, and, if there is truth in it, I will speedily take means to deliver him into the hands of justice.

" Ask me nothing upon that subject," replied the old woman, " for of him I neither can nor will speak, save that he has a soul too high and bold for what he seems."

" He seems to be a great favourite here."

" He is," she replied, " and not without reason, for the queen upon her throne has not a nobler heart, nor a hand more open and free, than this kindly Outlaw."

" Know you," asked Henry Neville, " what takes him so often into the neighbourhood of Holmwood Castle?"

" I suppose it is his humour," she replied, " as they say it is yours to be ever in the midst of strife and danger."

" Who has spoken to you of me?"

" The Outlaw himself."

" Ha! does he know me then?"

" I suppose he does," answered Dame Dagley ; " but whether or not I can take it upon myself to say that he would not utter a falsehood about you,"

" It seems he knows me then," exclaimed Henry Neville ; " yet where or when we have ever met before I have not the least recollection. But perhaps he only pretends a knowledge of me for purposes of his own."

" Recollect yourself before you make up your mind to that," answered the old woman. " Did he not call you by name when he held your hand from smiting my boy?"

" He did," exclaimed Neville, " but he that has heard my name has heard of the deeds that blazoned it. For my own part, I have no recollection of ever having seen the fellow till I met him last night beneath this roof."

" Does he belong to our party?" demanded Arnheim ; " for by Saint Peter and Saint Paul ! if he be a man of gentle blood, he must say whether he is for us or against us."

" At present," observed the Jesuit, " it would not be wise to put any man upon proof unless we were assured that he would rank himself as one of our party."

" In that respect he can act as he please," exclaimed Henry Neville ; " for I would not side with him even were he so minded. The man is my foe ; he hath thrust himself upon me ; and by intruding his weapon between me and my foe, robbed me of that high gratification the proud right of a conqueror."

" But your sword was up," answered Dame Dagley, " and there was no time for courtesies. You would have shown Martin no whit of mercy whilst your blood was warm. You would have slain him even in his father's house, where you had sought refuge from the storm."

" You know me not, Dame Dagley," exclaimed the young man. " My sword is as well governed as a war-horse is governed by the rein of his rider. The savage Arab can ride his courser against the spears of his comrades, and curb him within a hair's breadth of their points ; so can I guide my steel to the very breast of my foe, and make his life the dearer to him, as he has been the nearer to the line of his fate."

" It is easy to boast of what one can do," answered the old woman ; " but be that as it may, I beseech you let your revenge sleep, and, in place of bandying private quarrels and mere personal feuds, bend your daring souls to the work you have undertaken. Do that, gentleman, and it will afford you better opportunities of proving your courage. Your plot, I suppose, goes on prosperously?"

" It does."

" And in what way can I afford you assistance?"

" By obeying the directions I am about to give you," replied Henry Neville. " You are only required to give these two strangers shelter till night, when they will be able to remove themselves from hence to Holmwood Castle, where Sir Richard Langdale will give them a hearty welcome."

" Your bidding shall be obeyed."

" 'Tis well," he exclaimed ; " and now, dame, answer me one other question, and

I may perhaps see reason to pardon this outlaw the insolence he has been guilty of towards me. Is there any truth in the report that has reached my ears, that the base hind hath dared to whisper his vows of love in the ears of Blanche Landale ?"

"Go to! for I will not answer such a question," exclaimed the old woman. "His kindness to us, who have lived upon his bounty, would be well rewarded, truly, if I were to say aught against him. Would you have me injure one who has been to us a kind and generous friend ?"

"You will do as you please about it," answered Henry Neville; "but it is in my power to do more for you and your family than ever he has done."

"What can you do for us more than he has done ?"

"That remains to be proved hereafter," he replied; "but there are offices in my father's household that would suit both Martha and her brother."

"Ay, so there may be," exclaimed Dame Dagley; "but I would rather see them half fed and hungry as they are now, than have them decked out and pampered at the price of their mother's treachery. You cannot tempt me, young gentleman ;—all the wealth that your father possesses would fail to do it."

"Fool!" muttered Henry Neville; "I have offered you fairly, and my terms have been rejected. May the curse of everlasting poverty rest upon your stubborn folly."

"Ay, curse on," retorted the dame; "for the evil you wish shall not light upon me so soon as you think for ; and now, Henry Neville, hear the words of one who knows thy fate—the hand of Blanche Langdale, which thou hast so eagerly sought, shall never be thine."

"Woman, thou liest!" he exclaimed furiously; "for the hand of her thou hast named shall be mine ere another month has passed over my head. I have her father's word for it, and there are none others who have the power to control her."

"I am no witch," answered Dame Dagley, unmoved by the wrath she had excited; "but this I will say to thee, Henry Neville :—when thy fortune is at its flood, the triumph thou lookest for will be snatched from thy lips, and, instead of quaffing the ecstatic draught of intoxicating pleasure, thou wilt taste in all its bitterness the foul dregs of disappointment—the lees of despair, and shame, and ruin. Nay, frown not upon me thus, young sir, for, if my words have given you offence, it was yourself that urged me to give them utterance."

"Come, come, old hag," exclaimed Arnheim ; "by Saint Peter ! we'll have none of your fiend's tricks here. Cease this cursing, Mother Dagley, or this poniard of mine shall soon put an end to all your sorcery and whichcraft."

And as a proof that the threat had been uttered in earnest, the German threw aside his cloak and half drew from its sheath a dagger that he wore concealed there.

"Nay," interposed the priest, "govern thy passion, friend, and do not war against a helpless woman. We have higher deeds to accomplish than this, and all our plans may be thwarted if this foolish quarrel is carried any further."

"Eternal curses seize her !" muttered Henry Neville, in accents of the most ungovernable rage.

"Ay," she exclaimed, "give free vent to thy malice, young man, but know that thy curses are weak and powerless against her whom thou wouldst denounce. I am safe from them, Henry Neville ; for, unlike thee, I have not wantonly shed the blood of the innocent."

"Vile hag !" he cried, " darest thou say I have been guilty of murder ?"

"No," she replied scornfully, " nor art thou a robber and a plunderer, nor a committer of sacrilege, nor a fierce brawler and ruffian, nor a ravisher, nor—"

"Ha !—fiend !—sorceress!" exclaimed the other vehemently ; " who hath told thee these shameless lies ? Speak, woman, or I'll bury my dagger in your heart."

As he uttered this threat, Henry Neville grasped Dame Dagley by the throat, and, drawing forth his poniard, held it threateningly against her. Alarmed at what was passing, Arnheim and the priest advanced to prevent further violence, when cottage door was violently burst open, and Martin Dagley, accompanied by his father, rushed in, each armed with a sword. The latter struck the uplifted weapon from Neville's hand, and presented his sword at his breast. In the mean time Martin keep the priest and the German at bay.

"What is the meaning of this violence being offered against an old and helpless woman?" demanded the elder woodman. "Would you reward the hospitality with which we last night received you beneath our roof, by slaying my wife?"

"Had your wife been less irritating, there would have been no violence to complain of," answered Neville, moodily. "I came here on business of my own, and little thought of being engaged in a quarrel with a female. However, my anger is now over, so you need not fear any further violence, unless she is the first to provoke it."

"Your business, young sir, seems to be very mysterious," said Stephen Dagley, looking suspiciously at the two strangers, who had arrived during his absence from home.

"To *you*, it may appear mysterious," answered Henry Neville, "and yet there is nothing in it that need create either suspicion or distrust. We are friends together, and our meeting here was by a mere accident."

"They are foreigners, if I'm not mistaken."

"We are," answered the Jesuit; we knew the young gentleman abroad, and having just arrived in England followed him to this place to consult with him upon affairs that concern no one but ourselves."

"I don't want to know any of your secrets," exclaimed Stephen Dagley; "but I've a notion that you are a Roman Catholic priest, and, if that's the case, your presence in this country bodes no good to us."

"Why so, my friend?"

"Because there's a law to forbid all such persons coming from abroad to settle in this country."

"You are mistaken, old man," exclaimed the German, "as to what we are and the motive that has brought us here. We have private business in this country, and surely there is no crime in a man coming to visit a friend, even though he may happen to be a Catholic."

"I don't want to know what your business may be," answered Stephen Dagley, "but I've a right to suspect there's something evil going forward when you meet at a lonely, out-of-the-way place like my poor cottage. If you wanted to see Master Henry Neville, he was to have been found at the castle, and you might have followed him there without fear of meeting with a cool reception from Sir Richard Langdale."

"My friends were on their road there when they called to rest themselves at your cottage," exclaimed Neville. "By your wife, they were received with hospitality, and we should have departed well pleased with our reception, but for some angry words that she gave utterance to just as we were about to take our leave."

"I suppose, then, she took offence at something or another that I ought to resent?"

"There's nothing at all that it concerns you to know," cried Dame Dagley, anxious to suppress all further inquiries upon a subject which, for the present, she wished to remain secret. "I was, perhaps, over warm at some remarks that were made about the Outlaw, and one word brought up another, till we got into the wrangle that you came just in time to put an end to."

"Well, if no harm was meant, I shall say no more about it," returned the old man; "but I've a notion there's something wrong going on, and so I give fair notice that it's my intention to keep a sharp look-out to prevent mischief, if there should be any intended."

"There's nothing going on that we should be afraid of your knowing," answered Henry Neville; "but as they are family affairs, I do not feel inclined to trust them to the keeping of any other persons than ourselves."

" Do family affairs oblige you to speak against the poor, houseless stranger that sometimes finds a shelter beneath our roof?" demanded the woodman.

" If you mean the Outlaw," answered Henry Neville, " I have no inclination to interfere with him, so long as he refrains from thrusting himself in my way."

" Has he ever done so?"

" Report belies him else," exclaimed the young man; " for it is said he seeks the hand of Blanche Langdale, and, should he succeed, I lose both the maiden and the rich dower she is to receive on the day of her marriage."

" Oh! ho! there's jealousy in the affair, then?"

" Jealousy!" exclaimed Henry Neville. " Can it be supposed that I am jealous of one who, at any moment, I have the power to crush? He is a proclaimed outlaw, and, as such, it is your duty to give him up to justice, rather than give shelter to a felon."

" Call him felon or what you may," retorted Dame Dagley, " he has more honour than those who, for paltry motives of their own, seek to injure him. He is not what he seems, and you may take my word for it that the day will come when his enemies will be forced to acknowledge that he has been unjustly accused of evil doing."

" Perhaps," sneered Neville, " you are so great a favourite that he has intrusted you with the secret of who he is?"

" I have never been bold enough to ask him the question," answered Dame Dagley; " and he you speak of has too much prudence to trust the secret where he is not certain of its being safe. However, let it suffice that we believe him to be an innocent and persecuted man, and our doors will never be closed against him whilst he requires the shelter we are able to give him."

" Then before long you may be forced to surrender him up," exclaimed Henry Neville; " for it is suspected that he has taken refuge in this forest, and troops may soon be sent to hunt him like a wild beast from his lair."

" And perhaps," said the dame, significantly, " the same troops may have orders to look after certain traitors, who are not lurking very far from the forest. The soldiers will no doubt come here to look for the Outlaw, and, if he should be taken, there are certain other parties who may be sure that they will not remain at liberty much longer."

" Woman!" exclaimed the Jesuit, " you are speaking of matters that have nothing to do with the affair we have been talking about. Neither myself nor my friends have any desire to interfere with this Outlaw, nor do we know anything about the traitors, if any there be, that are to be found in this neighbourhood."

" So much the better," observed Stephen Dagley, " for I have always been a loyal subject of her majesty, and if I knew of any treason going on, I'd give the scoundrel up to justice, even if my own son was one among the number."

" When you have good grounds for believing the crown is endangered, it will be time enough for you to give proof of your boasted loyalty," exclaimed Henry Neville. " At any rate, all those who are here present are faithful subjects of Queen Elizabeth, and with that assurance I shall now take my leave. My friends, however, with your permission, will remain here for a brief time longer, and will then repair to Holmwood Castle, where they will be sure to receive a hospitable reception from Sir Richard Langdale."

Having, as he believed, put at rest the suspicions of the old woodman, Henry Neville quitted the cottage, in order to inform Sir Richard of the arrival of their new confederates. Stephen watched the retiring form of the young man with suspicion, and, when he had disappeared in the distance, he took up his woodman's axe and followed Neville, though at a sufficient distance not to be seen.

CHAPTER V.

Some fight, 'tis for riches; some fight, 'tis for fame :
The first I despise, and the last is a name.
I fight, 'tis for vengeance! I love to see flow,
At the stroke of my sabre, the life of my foe.—L. E. L.

DAY was drawing towards a close when Henry Neville left the woodman's cottage, and at that time the Outlaw had quitted the cave where he frequently concealed himself, intending, as soon as it was sufficiently dark, to take his customary walk towards Holmwood Castle, to obtain a stolen interview with Blanche Langdale. Under any other circumstances he would have scorned the secresy he was now obliged to observe, but the ban of authority had been proclaimed against him, and he must either consent to meet his mistress clandestinely, or lose all chance of gaining the beauteous prize, in the event of his love coming to the knowledge of her imperious father.

It is perfectly true that he was not conscious of any unworthy act that had been committed to bring upon himself the persecution he had endured; he had ever been faithful and loyal to his sovereign, had fought bravely in the cause of his country, and had won praise from those who were now loudest in their outcries against him. Yet, in spite of his hitherto blameless life, he had fallen under a conspiracy that had been formed against him, and so fiercely had the storm raged against him, that he had been compelled to flee from his home, and seek a temporary refuge in the ancient forest of Sherwood. But his proud spirit sometimes rose against the course he had adopted: he longed to venture from his wild retreat, and dare his enemies to prove their foul aspersions, and it is probable that he would ere now have surrendered himself into the hands of his enemies, but for the earnest prayer and supplications of Blanche Langdale, who feared that such a step would lead to his irrevocable ruin. For her sake, then, it was that he consented to lead the life of a fugitive and a wanderer, but though he did so in deference to her request, he looked forward to the time, which perhaps might not be far distant, when he might challenge the utmost malice of his foes to prove the charges they had brought against him.

On the evening to which we have alluded, he was more than usually pensive, for the arrival of Henry Neville at the castle had filled his mind with gloomy apprehensions—not that he was afraid of Blanche proving unfaithful to the vows she had so often uttered, but that he had heard her speak of her father's determination to insist upon her marriage with his young friend; and he believed there was too much reason to fear that she would be obliged to yield to the all-powerful commands of filial obedience. For the first time his heart failed him, as thought after thought chased each other through his mind, and as he wandered, almost unconscious where he was, he gave way more and more to the despondency that had taken possession of him.

"Ay," he at length murmured, as the rising moon just showed herself above the horizon, "'tis now near the hour when custom guides my footsteps to the castle glade, where, concealed by the favouring shades of evening, I hold sweet converse with my gentle Blanche. Yet I know not why it is, but a sort of instinctive dread fills my soul, and which the presence of this stranger, this Henry Neville, serves only to increase. He is my rival, my foe, and something tells me that a feud is about to rise between us, which will end only with the death of one or perhaps both of us. But hark!" he added, suddenly pausing, "footsteps are approaching this way. By Heavens 'tis he! the very man whom, of all others I would have most avoided meeting!"

Had he tried to avoid an interview it would have been impossible, for Neville had already perceived him, and, advancing hastily, he exclaimed, in a tone of triumph—

"In all my hopes, this meeting between us, sir, is most opportune. I have but just escaped the murderous assault of your friend Stephen Dagley, and now, when passion still rages in my heart, the foe I most hate stands within reach of my sword!"

"What would you with me?" demanded the Outlaw, turning, as if still bent upon continuing his way.

"Thou mayest pretty well guess what I want with thee," answered the other. "By my faith, sirrah, thou must still be dreaming of the saintly Blanche Langdale, or thou wouldst know that he who stands before thee is the foe who has sworn to shed thy blood."

"That is," replied the Outlaw, "if my skill in swordmanship is inferior to your own."

"True; but that will soon be put to the proof, and a short time will serve to convince thee that I have some of the devil's feelings of revenge about me."

"If thou art not the Great Fiend himself," answered the Outlaw, "thou hast, at least, all his attributes, for of honour thou hast none."

"Humph! thou art plain spoken at any rate, and so far I like thee somewhat better than I did."

"I ask for no favourable opinion of one whom I despise from my very soul," exclaimed the Outlaw. "I have seen little of you, Henry Neville, nor do I wish for further acquaintance with a man who can lay no claim to honour."

"Pshaw! What mean you by that same word *honour?*" demanded Neville. "How high does thine honour reach? canst thou measure it? does it reach to the altitude of yonder pine-tree that rises darkly against the moon-lit horizon? Or is it as broad as the river in which, Narcissus-like, thou, for want of a looking-glass, surveyest thine own exquisite countenance? Canst thou grasp thine honour in thy hand, or put it into thy pocket? *Honour!* didst thou ever hear of it in an outlaw?"

"Wert thou armed," exclaimed the other, "I would tell thee, Henry Neville, that I wear my honour in my scabbard. At present, therefore, I will take, or, at least, I will resent no insult that you can offer me."

"Thou resent!" returned the other scornfully. "Why, I would fight with thee even though I was armed with no better weapon against thy rapier but a bulrush from yonder sluggish brook. Thou hast tempted my wrath, and thus do I punish thine insolence!"

Bursting with fury, Henry Neville made a sudden spring forward and seized the Outlaw in his grasp. The latter, however, after a few violent efforts, hurled his adversary to the ground, and then, drawing his sword, stood over him in a threatening attitude, and, as a grim smile passed over his countenance, he exclaimed—

"Your life, young sir, is now, through your own folly, in my power. I have been threatened and bullied, and it is well for you that I am able to control the fiercer passions that you might have called up. Rise, sir, I ask for no concessions; but, after what has passed, it is better that we part without further quarrel. Leave me, young man, and from this time forth let us avoid each other."

Acting upon this hint, Henry Neville rose from his recumbent position, and, plucking out his dagger, threw himself into an attitude of defence.

"Thou hast braved me!" he exclaimed, hoarse with rage; "now, if thou art what thou dost profess to be—a man of blood and courage—throw down thy sword and let us engage fairly with each other at the dagger's point."

"Why should I do so, when I have already said that I am not just now in the humour to accept thy challenge?"

"Coward!" exclaimed Neville; "I now see that thou lackest the courage thou hast boasted of possessing."

"I make no boast of my courage," answered the Outlaw; "but you have proposed a way of settling our dispute, sir, that I am proud to say I have never yet practised. A dagger is a coward's weapon that I never carry."

"This is a paltry equivocation that will not serve thy purpose," exclaimed Henry Neville. "If thou hast courage enough to pursue this quarrel to an end, break thy sword to my dagger's length, and if it should appear that I have more point than thou hast, give me thy weapon and I will let thee have mine instead of it."

"Pshaw! are you mad to urge me thus against my own wish?"

"You refuse my terms!" exclaimed Henry Neville with increasing vehemence; nay, then, it seems I have done thee too much courtesy, for thou art unworthy to combat with one who prides himself upon his honour."

"What dost thou think me?" demanded the other, still unmoved by the violence of his foe.

"I know thee now," answered Neville, "to be a fellow as destitute of courage as of reputation. Thou art under a proclamation of outlawry, and for aught I know thou mayst have been guilty of crimes that render thee unworthy the challenge I have just offered."

No. 5.

" It is fortunate for thee, young man," answered the other, "that I can bear more now than even thy villanous slanders can lay upon me : I have learned in the school of adversity to govern my passions and never to give loose to them except in cases of extremity."

" A mere excuse to cover your cowardice."

" Call it what you please," exclaimed the Outlaw, " but I tell you, Henry Neville, for as bold and insolent as you have proved yourself this day, there is not one word of thine that shall fall to the ground unheeded : I will hoard thine insolence in my memory, and, when time serves, will repay it to thee with ample interest."

" I am glad to hear thou hast some spirit in thee," answered Henry Neville sneeringly ; " and I prithee, sirrah, do not take a long day to think of it, like some of our gallants, who wilfully neglect the reckoning till they believe all remembrance of the quarrel is buried in oblivion."

" I will at least prove to thee that I am no coward," retorted the Outlaw. "To-day I have refrained from using the means I possess to punish thee, but the time may come when you will repent the course you have adopted against me."

" Beware lest I deprive you of the power you boast of."

" You would take me when I am unprepared for your attack, I suppose," exclaimed the Outlaw ; "but do not imagine that the advantage is to be easily gained. If thou dost set upon me suddenly, thou wilt always find me armed and ready for the emergency. If thou dost use foul means, the dishonour will rest upon your own head."

" What dishonour can there be," demanded the other, " in seeking to capture or destroy one who has been denounced by royal proclamation, and whose life has already been forfeited to the offended laws of his country ?"

" As an innocent man," exclaimed the Outlaw, " I dare stand up and openly defy my enemies to prove any of the foul charges they have brought against me."

" Then why hast thou not done so before, instead of hiding thyself from those who are in pursuit of thee ?"

" My reasons will be satisfactorily explained when the proper time and opportunity arrive," answered the Outlaw haughtily. " I have now told thee as much as I intend to do at present, and it only remains for me to repeat, that any foul attempt to surprise me will, of a surety, recoil upon yourself."

" Nay, there is no reason to suspect me of treachery," answered Henry Neville; " for I will fairly meet thee with my sword, and no other weapon. Thou art now, if I mistake not, about to visit thy mistress, the fair Blanche Langdale, of Holmwood Castle. Thou art on thy way to her, and thou hadst best take thy last look of the maiden, for when we next meet thy doom will be surely sealed."

" Thou art a vain and insolent boaster," exclaimed the Outlaw ; " but the fate of our quarrel is not in thy hands. Thou mayst have to beg thy life of me, proud as thou art, and, should it ever be so, may Heaven inspire my heart with generosity enough to forgive a haughty foe. But the hour is at hand, as you say, when I pay my accustomed visit to the daughter of Sir Richard Langdale ; and remember, sir, if our interview is broken in upon, I shall not fail to punish him who intrudes himself into our presence."

" Your threats have very little effect upon one who despises them as heartily as I do," answered Henry Neville ; " I may, perhaps, be a listener to the tender things you have to say to the young lady, so I would have you be cautious how you urge your love, lest my rage should scorn all control, and I sacrifice you to my vengeance."

The Outlaw eyed him with a look of disdain as he replied,—

" You might have spared your threats, sir, since I have already told you that I shall always be prepared to resent either your interference or impertinence. I am the sworn champion of her you speak of, and am willing to lay down my life at any time in the defence of a woman who has honoured me as she has done with her confidence and regard."

" 'Tis false ! " exclaimed Neville ; " the maiden's confidence has been abused by a villain, and, backed as I am by the authority of her father, I will protect her from the snares you have laid for her destruction."

"Beware what you say, young man," cried the Outlaw, "for, though I have hitherto forborne to resent your insults, I may yet be urged to punish insolence when it passes beyond the bounds of endurance. However, I would avoid a quarrel, and therefore do I now leave you to reflect upon the folly of forcing the resentment which you may afterwards see reason to be sorry for."

The Outlaw spoke these words with more wrath than he had hitherto manifested, and, turning upon his heel, he made his way towards an adjoining thicket and immediately disappeared from the view of his infuriated antagonist. For a few moments Henry Neville stood as if irresolute what course to adopt; but at length, bursting with rage, he was about to follow his rival, when his arm was grasped by some one from behind, and, looking round, he encountered the fixed and earnest gaze of Stephen Dagley, the woodman.

"How now?" exclaimed the cotter; "what mad trick are you about to play against yonder man?"

"I would follow, to see where he is going," answered Neville, making a vain effort to extricate himself from the firm grasp of the person he would have avoided.

"So I fancied," exclaimed Stephen; "but as I've a notion that you have no very good purpose in view, I take the liberty of holding you my prisoner till I have your promise that no violence shall be offered to a man who it seems has already quite foes enough in this world to encounter."

"And if he has," cried Neville, "is that any reason why you should interfere between us? He has braved my anger, and I have a right to resent it as I think proper."

"All that may be true enough," answered the woodman, with apparent indifference; "but I happen to have overheard a great part of your conversation, and I am inclined to think he has more reason to complain than you have. From what I can understand, you are jealous of the preference shown him by Blanche Langdale, and to rid yourself of a rival you would not hesitate to murder him without just provocation."

"Have I not provocation enough, when I see him on the point of snatching from me the prize I most covet?" asked Henry Neville. "As an outlaw, he has sought refuge in this forest, and yet he would trepan an innocent maiden into the snares he has laid for her destruction."

"As for that, sir," exclaimed Stephen Dagley, "I am not quite certain that she would be worse off through marrying this mysterious stranger, than she would if she becomes the wife of a traitor to his queen and country."

"Hah!" exclaimed Neville; "what mean you by those words?"

"I mean neither more nor less than I have said," answered the woodman; "that there is a conspiracy hatching for the overthrow of our present sovereign, you know better than I do; but, humble and obscure as I am, you may rely upon it that there are those watching your actions who will thwart and counteract the project that has been formed."

"And you believe that I, as loyal a subject as is to be found in her majesty's dominions, am engaged in a treasonable plot against my liege sovereign?"

"If I was not pretty sure of it I should not have charged you so plainly with it," exclaimed the woodman. "I have no feeling of animosity against you, sir, nor shall I interfere so long as you trouble not your head with me."

"You are a most loyal and dutiful subject, certainly," retorted Neville; "for you believe me to be engaged in a conspiracy against the queen, yet will do nothing to prevent the mischief, on condition that I do not interfere to make known these secret meetings between yourself and the daughter of Sir Richard Langdale."

"If I remain passive," exclaimed the Outlaw, "it will not be to favour your treason, but to keep a watchful eye upon your actions."

"Yet the queen is no such great friend of yours that you need feel so much interest in her behalf."

"Her Majesty has been imposed upon by the artful reports of those who seek my destruction," answered the other: "men have been found base enough to pour their poison in the ear of my sovereign, and so successful have their efforts been, hat for a time I am compelled to seek safety in flight."

"Methinks it would have been better for an innocent man to confront boldly those whom he accuses of a design to plunge him into ruin."

"I have, myself, been almost tempted to do so," replied the Outlaw; "but of what use would be my own unsupported assertion against the combined efforts of those who have entered into this conspiracy against me? My denial would only provoke them to invent fresh falsehoods, and the chances are that they would succeed."

"And yet," exclaimed Henry Neville, "though you complain of the rumours that have been spread to your prejudice, you are willing to believe those that charge me with being in league with conspirators against the queen."

"The rumours you speak of would have passed unheeded but that I myself happen to have learnt sufficient to convince me that they are founded in truth."

"You have been acting the part of a spy then?"

"To a certain extent I plead guilty to the charge," answered the Outlaw ; "but if I have kept a watch upon your actions it has been to prevent a catastrophe that would bring anarchy and ruin upon the country. You would bring the country once more under the dominion of the Pope of Rome ; and all your animosity against the queen arises from the fact of her being a Protestant."

"You pretend to know much," exclaimed Henry Neville ; "yet, in this instance, you have shot wide of the mark."

"So you may try to convince me," returned the Outlaw ; "but my opinion is so well based that I dare accuse you, face to face, with being at the head of a band of conspirators whose object is to depose our monarch that you may place another of your own choosing on the throne of England."

"Indeed ! and who has told you this ?"

"My authority will be produced at the fitting time," answered the Outlaw.

'You speak of my being at the head of a band of conspirators; can you tell me the names of those who act under me ?"

'Two or three of them are not far off from us at the present time," replied the Outlaw. "One of them is Sir Richard Langdale ; the others have only just arrived, and are now to be found in the cottage of Stephen Dagley, the woodman."

"How !" exclaimed Neville, starting with surprise ; "do you suspect the two strangers of being concerned in this imaginary plot of yours ?"

"My suspicions amount almost to a certain conviction," replied the other ; "for I know more of them than you think for."

"What know you of them ?"

"That they are foreigners who have been tempted by English gold to do that which few of her Majesty's subjects would venture upon. One of them is a crafty Italian Jesuit priest, the other a German adventurer, who is willing to risk his life under a promise of being liberally rewarded in the event of the plot turning out successful."

"Humph ! this is mere guess-work of yours to frighten us into an offer to bribe you to silence."

"Nay," exclaimed the Outlaw, "I can tell you their names if you desire proof that I am guided by something more than guess-work. The priest is called Father Francis, and the other is known as Arnheim, though whether those are their real names is more than I will undertake to assert."

"You seem to have been at some pains to pry into affairs that concern you not," exclaimed Henry Neville. "Had I been aware that you were making yourself so busy with my affairs, I should have taken means to prevent your being so inquisitive into a matter that concerns you not. As it is, I have heard quite enough to prove that you are a dangerous enemy, and, before many hours have passed, I shall take care to prevent the mischief you may intend to do me."

"Your threat is a vain one, young man," answered the Outlaw; "for, in s ength, at least, I am your match, and, if no unfair advantage is taken, I believe my courage will be found in no way inferior to your own."

" Let us say no more about this," exclaimed Henry Neville ; "for neither you nor I shall get any good by quarrelling at a time like this. You have little reason to continue loyal to her who now fills the throne, and, if you will assist us in removing Elizabeth from her present exalted situation, I can, in the name of my friends, promise you a large reward for your services."

" So you acknowledge, then, that my suspicions are not altogether without foundation ?"

" I acknowledge nothing," answered the young man ; " though I do not deny the existence of a plot to counteract the heresy that was introduced into this country by Henry the Eighth. The cause in which we have embarked is a sacred one ; and, whether we succeed or fail, I shall never regret the part I have taken in my endeavours to bring back the nation to the religion which was followed by our forefathers."

" But you do it at your own hazard," exclaimed the Outlaw ; " for should there be any attempt to dethrone the queen, a discovery is certain to take place, and all those who have been concerned in the plot will perish on the scaffold as traitors to their country."

" I am not so blind as to be ignorant of that," returned Neville ; " but if I thought the discovery would be made through you I would force you to draw your weapon, and either you or I, or perhaps both of us, would perish on the scene of strife."

" Have I not said that I will not be urged into either giving or resenting an insult ?" exclaimed the Outlaw. " You have tried to urge on a quarrel, but I know the advantage to be all on my own side, and have no inclination to make use of it while there is a chance of your seeing the danger into which you are wilfully rushing. You may yet save yourself, Henry Neville, but it must be by abandoning this treasonable project, and avoiding the society of those men whom you have lately admitted to your confidence."

" Keep your advice for those who need it more than I do !" exclaimed the other scornfully. " I have not entered into this affair without giving it due consideration, and, whether good or evil comes of it, I am content to take whatever chance may come. As for my friends, they are not less zealous in the cause than I am myself; and, even though I might desert them like a coward at the eleventh hour, they would boldly carry it on, certain of bringing their project to a successful termination."

" Then I will see Sir Richard Langdale, and try if there is any way to save him from the peril he is threatened with."

" Sir Richard needs no advice that you can give him," answered the young man ; " for he is as resolute in the cause as the best among us, and his fortune, large as it is, has been placed at the disposal of those who are engaged with him. You see I am candid enough to admit that there is such a plot as you speak of in progress, but I should have hesitated to do so had I not been certain that you dare not reveal it."

" What is to hinder my doing so ?" demanded the Outlaw.

" The love, real or pretended, that you feel for Blanche Langdale is the safeguard upon which I depend," answered Neville. " The maiden is devotedly attached to her father, and never would she forgive the man who gave him into the hands of his enemies."

" But she knows nothing of the dangerous plot in which he is engaged with you."

" Perhaps not," answered Henry Neville;" but she would soon know of it though if you were to denounce those who are engaged in it. Hitherto her father has always been considered a faithful subject of Queen Elizabeth ; and he would have been so but for the anxiety he feels to see the old religion again flourishing in the country. I myself have no ill-feeling against the person of our sovereign, though I care not what length I go in order to root out the heresy that she countenances and supports."

" Yet her Majesty only follows the creed in which she has been brought up and educated."

" That may be," exclaimed Henry Neville, " but those who adhere to the old form of worship are not the better satisfied with her on that account. We who own the supremacy of the Pope know full well that, if the blow is struck at all, there is no time to be lost, for the new form of worship is gaining ground, and if we neglect our duty now all hope of our succeeding will be at an end."

" I see how useless it is to argue with you upon this point," said the Outlaw, " and therefore I shall now leave you to reflect upon the danger you are bringing upon yourself. For my own part, I shall keep a close watch upon those who are engaged in the sedition ; and when I see that my longer silence would be criminal, I shall at once denounce you and all those with whom you are in league."

" If you do so it will be at your own peril," exclaimed Henry Neville, " for though some of us may chance to fall, there will be others left to take vengeance upon the cowardly villain who brought ruin on our party."

" Let them do with me as they please," answered the Outlaw, " for, if I perish, there is at least the consolation of knowing that it will be in a good cause."

" And you will also have the reflection that it was through your means that the father of Blanche Langdale was sent to end his days upon a public scaffold."

" I may yet be able to devise some scheme to withdraw him from this dangerous confederacy," answered the Outlaw. " That he has been led away through listening to the false representations of artful men I have no doubt, and I will presently see whether he is so blind to his own interest as to continue his support to your party when he comes seriously to reflect upon the danger into which he is rushing. If no other alternative should remain, I will inform Blanche of the plot that is in progress against the sovereign, and the love she bears towards him will, I am certain, prompt her to exert all her powers of persuasion to abandon his associates ere they involve him in the ruin they are themselves so madly seeking."

Without waiting to hear any reply to this, the Outlaw turned away, and, plunging into a thicket, soon disappeared from view. Henry Neville would have followed him, but another project just then crossed his mind, and, anxiously reflecting upon his new scheme, he took a more circuitous route that led towards the ancient seat of Sir Richard Langdale.

CHAPTER VI.

So, sweeter than the feverish glare of day
Is meek and pensive evening's sober ray,
When the sad bird begins to charm the vales,
And earth revives beneath the cooling gales.—REV. E. HAMLEY.

On the evening of the interview described in the last chapter, Nicodemus Dove became restless and fidgety, and, not having yet seen anything of Catherine Langdale, and guessing that she had gone with her sister to meet the Outlaw, he stole forth from the castle in the hope of meeting with them. He was, however, doomed to be grievously disappointed, for, though he wandered round and round for nearly an hour, the young ladies made not their appearance, and the rising moon suggested to him a notion that it was not an hour when females should be absent from home, especially considering the sort of person they were gone to meet. Tired at last of his unsuccessful search, he retraced his steps towards the castle, muttering to himself all the way he went, the rambling thoughts that were just then passing through his mind :—

" By Jove !" he exclaimed. " this is a most poetical situation, truly, for a respectable middle-aged gentleman like myself to be found in ! Here am I, wandering and strolling about by moonlight, like a cat in search of his sweetheart, instead of being in the company of Catherine, who, I verily believe, intends, after all, to jilt me : but let her mind what she's about, for, if any tricks are played, I shall inform Sir Richard of the goings on, and then there'll be a very pretty rumpus, that will end in the Outlaw's being sent to jail, and Blanche going off into hysterics for the fate of her lover. But it will be no fault of mine, whatever may happen, for the girls should learn to keep better company, and not to neglect their father's visitor, who, by the bye, has met with but a sorry reception, and has not been favoured with the sight of one of the family since his arrival at the castle. I declare I begin to feel half sorry that I ever set out on this journey, and if my prospects don't mend by to-morrow I shall begin to think it's high time to take my departure, and leave Harry Neville to the unsociable people we've come among: and yet why should I give way to melancholy thoughts, when the night is so lovely, and the moon shining above like——By the bye—talking of the moon, what a magnificent subject that would be for a poem!—so original too, that I dare say no one has ever thought of writing about it. Let me see if I couldn't do something that will astonish Neville, in spite of his always showing such impatience when I indulge in my poetic fancies. I'll begin it thus :—

> " Refulgent planet, sailing round about,
> Oh, when you shine the little stars go out !
> I sing your praise——"

Here the poet's inspiration was brought to a sudden standstill by the sound of a guitar, accompanied by the voice of the Outlaw. It was in vain that he looked for the singer, for he had concealed himself amidst a cluster of trees; but on directing his eyes towards the chamber of Blanche, he saw her standing at the widow, and making signs to the serenader, as if to warn him of the presence of another person. In an instant the music ceased, and, as it did so, the young lady disappeared from the window.

"By Apollo!" muttered Nicodemus Dove, "some one else seems inclined to sing the praises of the moon as well as myself; and, if I'm not mistaken, the voice was that of the mysterious Outlaw that calls himself the rival of Henry Neville. Well, never mind, he don't come after Catherine, that's pretty certain, so, instead of going in search of him, I'll just conceal myself behind this tree, and keep watch upon my gentleman's actions. He may be going to run away with the young lady, and if so, I'll prevent the elopement, and thus earn the eternal gratitude of my intended father-in-law."

In pursuance of this design, Nicodemus immediately sought the shelter he had spoken of; and scarcely had he done so when other voices were heard, and in a moment or two afterwards Sir Richard Langdale and Henry Neville approached the place where the poet was concealed, and from whence he could hear all that passed.

"This, Sir Richard," observed the latter, "is somewhere near the spot from whence came the sounds of music that we just now heard. I have no doubt the guitar-player was no less a personage than this mysterious Outlaw, and, if my suspicions are correct, I will not return to the castle till I have punished the audacity that brought him here."

"The punishment of the scoundrel must be left to myself," exclaimed the baronet, "for he has dared to pay his stolen address to my daughter, and I have sworn never to relax in my endeavours till I have brought him to a severe reckoning."

"That might be done without risking your life against his," returned Henry Neville. " There is a proclamation of outlawry against him ; and if you only give a hint that he is lurking about in your neighbourhood, a sufficient number of the military will be sent from Nottingham to make his capture both safe and certain."

"Granted, my dear Henry," exclaimed the other ; "but it's a cowardly way of vanquishing an enemy that I don't like. No, no, my arm has not yet lost its strength, nor is my heart deficient of any of its former courage, so I'll e'en meet sword's point to sword's point, and, if he should chance to prove the victor, I must leave my daughter to your brotherly protection."

" I myself owe him a grudge that will never be satisfied till we have met in mortal combat," answered Neville. "He has dared to become my rival for the affections of your daughter, and by Heaven! I'll——But, hark! I hear again the notes of his guitar; so do not stir, for he knows not of our presence here, and, doubtless, he is about to treat the too confiding Blanche to a serenade."

"It is impossible it can be the person you suspect," exclaimed Sir Richard; "for he knows the hatred I bear towards him, and would hardly be so venture-some as to come thus near to my castle."

"Who do you think it is then?"

"Some peasant, perhaps, returning from his labour."

"Peasants, Sir Richard, are not often such practiced players upon the guitar. However, before we leave this place, I dare say you will see reason to alter your opinion, and you will then own that it is time we take steps for getting rid of this mysterious intruder."

"I would give a hundred marks to know who he really is," exclaimed the baronet.

"Some person of mean and obscure birth, I'll be bound he is," returned Henry Neville; "but, whoever he may be, the fellow knows too much of our secrets; and if we do not take speedy means to be rid of him, we shall soon have reason to repent our want of caution."

"What does he know of our secrets?" asked Sir Richard Langdale with alarm.

"A great deal more than we could have desired," replied the other, "and quite enough to place us entirely at his mercy if he should think proper to make use of it against us. He is aware of our plot for dethroning the queen, and a word from him upon that subject would be sufficient to send us to the scaffold."

"That is bad hearing indeed!" exclaimed the baronet, "and yet I should hardly think we have much to fear from him, since he has not yet made use of the secret."

"There's a reason for his forbearance that I should have thought needed no explanation from me," answered Neville. "The truth is, he knows you are as deeply implicated in the conspiracy as any of us, and he would hardly reveal his knowledge of our designs with the certainty before him of sending the father of Blanche Langdale to an ignominious death."

"In that case," observed Sir Richard, "would it not be as well if we tried to enlist him in our cause?"

"It would be useless for you to make the attempt," answered Neville, for I have myself tried him upon that point, and my suggestions have been treated with scorn. He is still loyal to the queen in spite of the proclamation she has caused to be issued against him."

"How then are we to act in such a case?" asked the baronet. "As a foe he his most dangerous to us, and I would therefore try if we cannot obtain his friendship."

"By offering him your daughter's hand, I suppose!"

"No, that I will never do," answered Sir Richard. "You have already received my sanction to pay your addresses to her, and no danger that threatens shall ever induce me to forfeit my word. But I might offer him a shelter in my house till the search after him is over, and then, if we can prevail upon him to go abroad, we should get rid of a personage who it seems is likely to give us no little trouble."

"Surely, Sir Richard, you would not be mad enough to receive him beneath your roof!" exclaimed the young man. "Why, it would be holding out an encouragement to his passion for your daughter, and before long you would see reason enough to repent so incautious a step."

"I know not what to suggest nor how to act," cried the baronet in the utmost perplexity."

"I see you are unfit to act for yourself in a case of emergency like the present," answered Henry Neville; "so surrender all the power into my hands, and I will so manage matters that the difficulties you dread shall soon disappear."

"How will you do it?"

"Easily enough if I am left to myself," answered the other. "I have already had a quarrel with him that had nearly brought us to a trial of skill in swordsmanship, and when I left him a short time since it was with an understanding that I should take the first opportunity that offers to revenge myself for certain insulting expressions that he uttered against me."

"That was rash on your part, to say the least of it."

"And why was it rash, Sir Richard?"

"Because, if he knows as much of our secret as you say he does, he may denounce us for this affair, which, up to the present time, we had thought was known only to those who are concerned in the plot."

"We have nothing to fear from him on that account," returned Henry Neville, "for, to do him justice, he appears to have honour enough about him to prevent the chance of his becoming an informer."

No. 6.

" Then he can be no friend to the queen."

' I don't know anything about his being a friend to her Majesty," answered the young man, " but he seems to be quite satisfied with having it in his power to watch us till our plans are ripe for execution. Up to that point I know we are safe, and it therefore only remains for us to prevent his gaining any information that he may turn against us."

" Are you sure that all our people are to be depended on ?"

" I am quite certain they are."

" That is more than I can say myself," exclaimed Sir Richard Langdale, "for I like not your notions of bringing those two foreigners here, when, by a word, they have it in their power to ruin us, if it should be made to appear that their interest will be better served by betraying us to those against whom we are leagued."

" Pshaw !" returned Henry Neville, " do you think that I would have trusted the men if I had not first of all satisfied myself that they are worthy of our confidence ? They are foreigners, it is true, but they are also Catholics, and deep in their hatred against the heretics who have now all the power of government vested in their hands. In short, Sir Richard, they will soon be here, and you will then judge for yourself if my confidence in them has been misplaced."

" I hope they are not to remain here as visitors."

" What else is to be done with them ?" demanded Henry Neville. " As strangers their presence would excite too much notice in the neighbourhood, and perhaps that might lead to inquiries that might lead to consequences that it is our chief object to avoid."

" Cannot they remain at the cottage of Stephen Dagley ?"

" Not without danger," replied the other. " Stephen Dagley already suspects that they are here for no good purpose, and he is of too rough and unyielding a nature to be trusted with a secret upon which our lives depend. The woman, it is true, seems to have as much hatred towards the queen as we ourselves have ; but she may suffer her tongue to run too fast, and it would therefore be dangerous to let her know of the plot that is in progress."

" And how long do you think it will be before we are able to carry our designs into effect ?"

" That will depend entirely upon circumstances," answered Neville. " At present all things seem to be going on most favourably, and the arrival of these two foreigners will serve to hasten matters towards a close. A few days more will bring a communication from some of our friends in London, and when we know how they are going on we shall be able to decide upon the time when a general rising throughout England shall take place."

" But are you sure that none of the queen's party are aware of what is going on among us ?"

" It is impossible for me to answer that question," said Henry Neville ; " but if we may judge by what is going on at court, I should be inclined to say that hitherto our secret movements have not been observed. Indeed, had there been the slightest suspicion, we should have had some of the queen's body-guards among us before this time.'

" Don't make too sure on that account," replied the old man, " for they may be aware of what we are doing, and remain silent observers of our actions till the moment when we are about to strike the blow. Such things have been done before now, my friend, and we ought therefore to prepare ourselves for any sudden emergency that might happen to arise."

" Do you think," asked Neville, " that this Outlaw is passing himself here under an assumed character in order that he may the better worm himself into our secrets ? He is believed to be a fugitive from justice ; but a notion has just come into my head that he may have come into this neighbourhood for no other purpose than to be a spy upon our actions."

" There's no saying what his purpose may be," answered the baronet ; " but I have always believed him to be under the ban of the law, and so far I see no reason to alter my opinion. But, hark ! my daughter comes from the castle to meet her lover ; so retire with me, and we will watch them till we discover what motive they have in view."

Scarcely had they concealed themselves in the shadow of one of the bastions, when the lovers met, and, having first looked around them to see if they were observed, Blanche entreated the Outlaw to leave the neighbourhood at once in order to avoid the evil designs of Henry Neville, who she well knew had resolved upon his destruction.

"Nay, dearest," answered the other, "do not ask me to act the part of a coward, for sooner would I perish than flee from one whose malice I so much despise. That he would crush me I know, but he lacks the power to do so, and I can therefore remain near you with less danger to myself than you imagine."

"But he has sworn to hurl upon you the destruction that your foes so anxiously wish for."

"I have no doubt of his evil intentions," replied the Outlaw, "but fortunately I am not so completely in his power as you seem to imagine. I have, in short, little to fear from him, for, should I find myself too sorely pressed through his means, I have an easy method of ridding myself of so inveterate a foe. He is in my power, Blanche, and let him beware how he urges me too far, for, as Heaven is my witness, the villain shall perish if he seeks, by an act of perfidy, to surrender me into the hands of my enemies!"

"So you may believe," she replied ; "but, little as I know of him, I can see that he has the subtlety of a fiend about him, and, should you come to an open quarrel with him, I fear the advantage will be all on his side."

"As for that," answered the Outlaw, "I must take my chance when I have a crafty foe like him to deal with. But, at all events, I know more of his secret thoughts than he thinks I do ; and if I am urged too far, I may perhaps say and do that which will bring his head to the block."

"Is he a traitor then ?"

"What he is I shall not say at present," replied the Outlaw ; "all that I can explain is that Neville stands upon the brink of destruction, and a word from me would hurl him headlong down the fearful abyss. At present, however, dearest Blanche, I cannot explain myself further. I am here to-night to tell you that we shall be obliged to part ere long, and I could not leave the place till I had an assurance from your own lips that you will remain constant to those vows which you have so often made—to love none other than myself."

"You may leave me with a perfect assurance that my heart can never change its affection."

"That I am already certain of," he exclaimed ; "but your father is obstinately determined that you shall become the wife of my rival, and I sometimes fear lest you should be forced to yield to his commands."

"I will never be dragged an unwilling bride to the altar," answered Blanche Langdale, in a tone expressive of the most determined resolution. "My regard for thee cannot be changed at the command even of a parent ; and this night I have proved the sincerity of my affection by venturing to leave the castle, where a discovery of my absence would lead to results that I dread to think of."

"Nay, do not be alarmed on that account," said her lover, "for your father is himself absent to-night, and, as I think, will not return for some time."

"Ah !" sighed the maiden, "he is changed, sadly changed, since he has been in such frequent communication with Henry Neville ; his mind seems to be filled with gloomy thoughts ; and so changed are his manners to those whom he once loved that I sometimes fear he has yielded to evil counsels, which in the end will plunge him into ruin."

"Sir Richard Langdale has indeed fallen into the snare that has been craftily laid for him," exclaimed the Outlaw. "He blindly follows withersoever this Henry Neville chooses to lead him, and, unless some powerful arm is stretched forth for his rescue, I fear his fate is inevitable."

"And you know his danger," cried Blanche reproachfully, "yet have taken no means to save him."

"My life shall be sacrificed in his behalf should it be needed," answered the other; "but you know the hatred he bears towards me, and the impossibility of obtaining an interview in which I might persuade him against the mad scheme in which he is engaged. All I can do, Blanche, is to watch him, and should I see him about to fall I will make one desperate effort to rescue him at the risk of losing my own life."

"I will myself undertake the task of watching him," cried the maiden; "but I know not the nature of the business in which he is engaged, and therefore am not prepared with any plan by which his rescue may be effected. You know the secret, yet am I left to the torture of this most fearful suspense, knowing but too well that my father is in danger, but having neither the power nor the means to avert the peril that I dread to think of."

"Reproach me not, Blanche, if I have kept this a secret from you," exclaimed the Outlaw. "I have vowed within myself to keep it, and not even my love for you shall tempt me to break my resolution till all other means of saving him shall have failed."

"Does he know that you are aware of what is going on?"

"At present I believe he does not suspect it," replied her lover; "but this evening I told Henry Neville that I was acquainted with the purpose he has in view, and no doubt he will soon inform your father of what passed between us. What effect that will have remains to be proved. I hope it will deter them from their purpose, at least for the present, but if not it will then be for me to take whatever other steps may appear to be necessary."

"And I am not considered worthy to be trusted with a secret of this importance?"

"Do not blame me for what I have done, Blanche," he exclaimed; "for I know the filial affection with which you regard your father, and if I have remained silent upon this subject it is that I feared to make a disclosure that could have tended to no good purpose. I have myself undertaken to guard him from danger, and even if he should be standing on the very verge of destruction I believe it would be still in my power to rescue him."

"But if it should be left to the last moment," cried Blanche, "will it not lead to a discovery that will cover his name with eternal disgrace?"

"Not if he will listen to reason and withdraw his assistance before it is too late," answered the Outlaw. "I may, however, soon have an opportunity of speaking to him, and whenever that may be the case I shall not fail to point out to him the danger into which he is running himself. He will become alarmed when he discovers that I know all, and were he once to quit his associates I should feel little hesitation in giving up the others to the fate they justly deserve.'

At that moment Blanche uttered a wild shriek of alarm, and on looking round him the Outlaw perceived that Sir Richard Langdale and young Neville were standing within a few paces of them. It was in vain for him to attempt further concealment, and, as flight would be equally useless, he advanced with a bold front and demanded if they had taken the mean advantage of listening to their conversation."

"We have heard all that has passed," answered the baronet; "not one word has escaped us: and now that we are fully acquainted with your designs, I have come forward to thank you for the kindness you have professed towards me. I, however, need none of your care, though you had need look after yourself, for he who would rob me of my daughter has no mercy to expect from her justly incensed father."

"Leave this quarrel, Sir Richard, to be settled between him and myself," exclaimed Henry Neville; "for he would take from me the prize you are about to bestow upon me, and our swords shall decide to whom she is to belong. Draw, sirrah, if you lack not courage to defend yourself, for you leave not this spot till I have had the satisfaction I demand."

"In the presence of a female my sword leaves not its scabbard," exclaimed the Outlaw, as he surrendered the fainting girl into the arms of her father, who immediately bore her towards the castle. " I have borne with your insolence before now," he continued, "and shall do so on the present occasion because it suits my purpose. But remember, there may some day or another be a limit to my forbearance, and whenever I do accept your challenge, Henry Neville, the strife betwixt us will be a bloody one, for never will I yield whilst life or strength romains to me."

" Why not decide our quarrel now?" demanded the young man ;—" why omit an opportunity that is so favourable to us in every respect?"

" Because I have other purposes in view that must be accomplished ere I risk my life in this quarrel," answered the Outlaw.

" Pshaw! 'tis the mere excuse of a coward who fears the vengeance he has drawn upon himself."

" Your sarcasms will fail to urge me to accept your challenge at this moment," exclaimed the Outlaw. " You may call me coward if you will ; but traitor you never shall."

"Villain! this to thy heart then," vociferated Neville, making a sudden rush upon the Outlaw, who, however, parried the blow with apparently but a slight effort.

"You will find yourself no match for me in strength," he exclaimed ; "and even were my arm weaker than it is, I have those near me who would rush to my rescue the moment they find I am in danger. Be careful, therefore, how you pursue this quarrel further, for the advantage is all on my own side, and you may soon have reason bitterly to repent the ungovernable passion you have manifested on this occasion."

" I! insolent ruffian! am I to be schooled by thee ?"

" This meeting was not sought by myself," answered the Outlaw, " nor was I aware till a few minutes since that we had listeners so near to us. You have, however, played the part of an eavesdropper, and learning, as you must have done, the intention I have just expressed, you will act wisely in abandoning a conspiracy that can only end in your own discomfiture and disgrace."

" Keep your counsel, sirrah, for those who are more inclined to accept it than I am," cried Neville, scornfully. " I am well enough able to take care of myself ; but it yet remains a matter of doubt whether you will escape the punishment due to your crimes."

" I am not aware of having committed any."

"Then why have you been outlawed, and a reward offered for your appre·hension ?"

" That is as great a mystery to myself as it appears to be to you," answered the other. I have said before that I owe all my sufferings to the evil reports of secret foes ; but why they have sought my ruin I know not, since I am not aware of ever having injured any one, either by thought or act."

" 'Tis false!" exclaimed Neville ; " you would injure me because I happen to be in your power ; but I am resolved to thwart your malicious intentions, and before I leave this spot I will punish the treachery you intend."

" Be cautious, young man," exclaimed the Outlaw, " or you will soon repent this violence. I have already said that I am not without friends here, though you see them not, and the instant there appears to be occasion for it they will rush forth in my defence."

" Let them do so," answered Henry Neville, " for the baronet's retainers are also at hand ; so that there is likely to be a sanguinary conflict if once your friends interfere in our quarrel. We are deadly foes to each other, as well as rivals in love ; and as matters must come to a crisis between us sooner or later, it would be best that we settle our differences before we part."

" Have you considered well the danger to which you would expose yourself?'

" I have."

"Then you must be mad to risk your life in an act of violence that, end as it may, can but involve you in a dilemma from which there is no chance o escape. It may be my chance to fall in this quarrel ; but even if it should be so, your treason will be made manifest, and you need no hint from me that her Majesty will show no mercy to those who have been base enough to plot against her life."

"The stranger speaks truly," whispered Sir Richard Langdale; "and therefore do I counsel you to leave the settlement of this quarrel till another opportunity."

"And, in the mean time," muttered the other, "this fugitive outlaw is to be suffered to escape."

"There is no fear of my attempting to do that whilst Blanche Langdale continues in this neighbourhood," replied the person alluded to, who had caught the words which had just escaped from the lips of his rival. "She is the attraction that has held me here, and it is not any danger of my own that will banish me from her presence."

"In that case," exclaimed Sir Richard, "I will soon remove the attraction to some place which will not be easily discovered;—then, perhaps, you will quit our forest, which, by the bye, seems to be the only way that remains for you to escape the vigilance of those who are endeavouring to discover the place of your retreat."

"Am I to understand," demanded the Outlaw, "that your daughter is to be removed for no other reason than that she has bestowed her affections upon me?"

"Ay, and cause enough too in my opinion."

"Your precaution will be vain then," exclaimed the other; "for even should you resolve upon sending her from England, I will find means ere long to discover the place to which she may be conveyed."

"You hear the insolence of the villain," cried Henry Neville. "Yet am I forbidden to chastise him as he deserves! By my soul, Sir Richard, I cannot understand this forbearance towards one who is under sentence of outlawry, and against whose life it is the duty of all men to raise their arms."

"If you would learn the reason of your friend's forbearance, I will presently explain it," exclaimed the Outlaw. "He is himself a traitor against the queen and her government, and, as the secret is known to me, he is wise not to urge me to disclose the plot in which he is engaged. Remember, one word from me would be sufficient to procure my own pardon, whilst it would send him to end his life ingloriously on a scaffold."

"And you would take that course against the father of the maiden you profess to love?" cried Neville bitterly.

"Had I been inclined to do so," answered the other, "neither he nor you would have been at liberty. But I have no feelings of revenge to gratify, and would therefore wait till I see whether you may not abandon a conspiracy that can only terminate in your own destruction. Remember, however, that I shall never cease to watch your motions, and should there be occasion for it I will preserve the life of my sovereign even though it might place the father of Blanche Langdale in peril."

Having uttered this in a tone of firmness and decision, the Outlaw turned upon his heel and left them. Henry Neville would have followed to gratify the revengeful feelings that had taken possession of his heart, but the arm of Sir Richard Langdale stayed him, and with reluctance he accompanied the old man to his private apartment in the castle.

CHAPTER VII.

Shall I not claim authority o'er one
Who owes her life to me? By Heaven!
She either weds the husband of my choice,
Or from this hour I cast her off for ever.—THE KINSMEN.

AFTER a brief interval Sir Richard went to seek his daughter, in order to remonstrate with her upon the encouragement she gave the Outlaw, and Henry Neville proceeded to the chamber where Arnheim and Father Francis were impatiently waiting his appearance. In few words he explained to them the reason of his long absence, and having done this the German burst forth with his usual vehemence.

"And so," he exclaimed, "that teufel's dam, Mother Dagley, must needs turn against us when most her assistance was needed. She takes part with the Outlaw, does she? then it's time for us to look out, so I wonder you did not kill the old hag when you found out that she might do us a mischief."

"I wish I hadn't been such a fool as to hesitate," answered the young man; "but the truth is, I was afraid her death might put a stop to the other affair that we have got in hand."

"And then there's the Outlaw," observed Father Francis; "he his still alive to do us all the mischief he can, and you might easily have got rid of him if you had been so minded."

"I had my motives for forbearance."

"Oh! you are afraid of him, I suppose?"

"I am not afraid of him, if we should meet together in fair combat," answered Henry Neville; "but it must needs be confessed I have my suspicions that on the first offence he receives he may go and denounce us for this plot of ours against the queen. Now, however, he has roused my vengence, and I'll hunt him through the world but what I'll punish him for the taunts he has this night uttered. Neither woods, nor castles, nor sanctuaries shall shelter him now that my spirit has been roused."

"How came you to meet him to-night so near the castle?" demanded Father Francis.

"Can you not guess what brought him here?"

"Why, I suppose, if the truth was told, he came to visit the daughter of our host. You came suddenly upon the lovers in the midst of their conversation, and thence arose the quarrel of which you have been telling us."

"Right, holy father," exclaimed Henry Neville, "you might have supposed as much from the brief narrative I have given, but you shall know the whole story at some future opportunity. But hark! I hear the voice of Sir Richard Langdale in angry conversation with his daughter; he comes this way, but there is no need of an introduction, since he knows you from my report, as you do him."

He had scarcely done speaking when the baronet entered the room, dragging with him the reluctant and terrified Blanche. It seemed that all his remonstrances had failed to bring her to his own views, and dragging her towards a chair he exclaimed passionately,—

"Sit there, thou foul dishonour to my name; from henceforward I will not quit thee for so much as a single moment. My eyes shall rest upon thee and scare thy soul like the evil sight."

"I prithee, Sir Richard," interposed Neville, "withhold thine anger awhile, for we have business of the utmost importance to attend to. In short, these two gentlemen are the friends of whom I have spoken."

"As friends to the good cause in which we are engaged ye are both heartily welcome to my castle," exclaimed the baronet, suddenly forgetting the anger into which he had suffered herself to be betrayed. "Monsieur Arnheim, I am heartily rejoiced to see you. Father Francis, your presence is most welcome. You must excuse my delay in coming to give you the greeting of hospitality, but a misfortune has fallen upon my house, and that, I trust, will be all the apology you need for my seeming inattention."

"Nay, Sir Richard," answered the priest, "it does not become us to intrude in family matters; something, I see, has served to excite you, and, by your leave, we will retire till a more convenient opportunity."

"My friend," exclaimed the baronet, "there is no need for secresy, for the whole world shall witness the shame of this undutiful girl—this deceiver—this most unnatural daughter. Ay, wench, thou mayst weep for thy dishonour—weep out thy false heart and get thee a better, or thou art no longer a child of mine! Thy base-born lover must now fall into my power, for I have sent out parties in every direction, with strict orders that they are not to return till there is no longer a chance of capturing him."

"I entreat you, Sir Richard," interposed Henry Neville, with affected concern; "do not afflict the poor maiden with these heavy reproaches. It is I, rather, who have deep cause for anger, yet even I can overlook the past, and take her to my bosom as if nothing had occurred."

"What!" exclaimed the baronet suddenly; "wouldst thou still marry her?"

"Most assuredly I would."

"Can I indeed believe thee?" demanded Sir Richard; "wouldst thou—shamed and blurred as she is—spotted and disgraced—accept her for thy wife?"

"Ay," answered Henry Neville, "and esteem myself blessed by so precious a gift."

"Then take her," exclaimed the baronet; "she is thine, my friend. Blanche, give him your hand, for in Henry Neville you behold your future husband."

"Oh! no, no," she cried, in an agony of terror, "he shall never be my husband. Cast me off—disclaim me—forget I ever drew the breath of life—let me live in misery and contempt—I will bear all rather than become the wife of that traitor, Henry Neville!"

"What!" exclaimed her father sharply; "darest thou, girl, to cavil at my words?"

"Nay, I would but reason with thee."

"I will hear none of thy reasons," he exclaimed. "I charge thee, Blanche, do not anger me beyond the power of control. Thou seest I am already somewhat heated with passion."

"Heaven knows I would spare myself your reproaches, were it possible," she replied; "I would obey you if I could, but my mind is resolved, and, be the consequences of my refusal what they may, I will not marry Henry Neville."

"Nor will I ask thee again to do so," exclaimed her father, with renewed passion. "I have resolved upon this marriage, and when thou art questioned about it again it shall be by the priest at the altar."

"And I," cried Blanche, in a tone of firmness and resolution, "will answer solemnly 'No!'"

"Wilt thou reveal to me,' demanded her father, "the name of thy recreant lover?"

"I pray you, sir, question me no further upon that subject," cried Blanche, "for, were I to reveal that secret, I should but prove myself more base and abject than you have already said I am. I will deny nothing which you may have seen or heard, but more the most cruel tortures you can inflict shall not wring from me."

"Then I have done with thee for ever," exclaimed her incensed father. "Thou art no more a child of mine: I will but be thy jailor till thou art married to this noble youth; then let him look to the taming of thy rebellious spirit. So, come with me to thy chamber, which for a brief period must be thy prison. Gentlemen, pardon me for the present, whilst I see to the safe custody of my charge."

He immediately withdrew, dragging with him his unresisting daughter; and the German, filling another glass of wine from the bottle that stood before him, exclaimed,—

"Our worthy host needs make no apology, for I shall not stir till we have drunk off the remainder of this excellent sack. The draught is a delicious one, and I have sworn to drain every bottle in honour of our host, whose hospitality has made us welcome."

"Psha!" remonstrated Henry Neville; "why, thou hast surely drunk enough for to-night. Three bottles hast thou already swilled since sitting here, and how many before, Heaven only knows."

"Come, Arnheim," interposed the priest, "our young friend would keep thee sober, and I would fain aid him in so prudent an undertaking. Let us retire to rest, for to-morrow morning there will be much work for us to do."

No. 7.

"Retire to rest!" exclaimed Arnheim, in a tone that indicated approaching intoxication. I am not yet sleepy, old friend, nor am I weary, except of the impertinence of my two pretended friends. And thou, Harry Neville, art as milky a sop at a cup of wine as ever told a long story to save his liver. Sit ye down, gentlemen, sit ye down; never part a man and his liquor. So here's a toast for the success of our cause! Drink, sirs, or on the word of a soldier I'll switch ye both with my sword-belt."

"Curse your toast," muttered Henry Neville; "I'm in no humour for swaggering, so hold your tongue, Arnheim, or we shall not be friends much longer."

The German started from his seat at these words, and, as he drew forth his dagger, exclaimed,—

"May I be carried off by a broken lance—may I be cut down by a suttler if I put up with this insult! Curse my toast, but I'll wash out this insult in thy blood. I challenge thee to mortal combat, and if thou dost not accept it, I will write thee a coward and a dog on every post in England."

"Thou shalt not waste thy time," retorted Henry Neville, drawing his rapier; "thou seest I am ready for thee, but lay aside thy dagger; point to point in fair duel, and thy weapon is longest too,—measure for measure. Father Francis, do us the favour to compare our weapons, and then take this gentleman's dagger into thy keeping."

He made a sign to the priest, who immediately approached and took the weapon, as if for the purpose of comparing them. Having got them in his hands, however, he directed his steps towards the door, which, having opened, he said,—

"With your leave, gentlemen, I'll retire, and take with me your weapons; for as a man of peace, it is my duty to prevent the bloodshed that your unseemly violence portends."

"Father Francis, you will before long repent this interference," exclaimed the enraged soldier. "This quarrel between Henry Neville and myself can end only with the life of one of us, and though you have deprived me of my weapons I will soon supply myself with others, and being once more armed, this stripling shall feel the weight of the anger his insolence has provoked."

"Nay," answered the Jesuit, "there is little fear of that, for when your brain becomes cool you will see the madness of pursuing your quarrel at a time like this. We have need of all our caution, or the cause in which we are engaged will be lost, and our own lives sacrificed to your want of discretion. So for the present, Captain Arnheim, I bid you farewell, and when we meet again in the morning, I hope to find you in a less intractable mood than you are at present."

And so saying the priest withdrew himself from the room, leaving his two friends to reconcile themselves to each other in the best way they could. The German was over-boiling with rage at the defeat he had sustained, but Henry Neville, who had more command over himself, treated the matter with apparent indifference, and advancing to follow the priest, he exclaimed,—

"I leave you, Captain Arnheim, to the free indulgence of your own reflections, and may you, as the effects of your intemperance wear off, become a more rational man. I now go to the cottage of Dame Dagley, and if my present mind hold good till I reach it, two hours hence shall not see one stone standing upon another."

"What good can you expect from pursuing your vengeance against a helpless woman?" demanded the German.

"Question me not as to my motives or my expectations," answered Neville; "but let it suffice thee to know that I have doomed her to destruction, and when once my heart and soul are set upon an object, neither the remonstrances of my friends nor the certainty of my own danger are of any avail to turn me from my purpose."

"Ugh!" muttered Arnheim, "and all the ill-feeling arises, I suppose, from her having taken part with the Outlaw?"

"That is the principal cause," replied the other, "but it matters little why I am resolved upon her destruction, since nothing can save her from the wrath she has provoked."

"My brain is not very clear after the sack I've swallowed since we've been sitting here," exclaimed Arnheim; "but muddled as I am, I can foresee danger from this mad freak of yours. Leave the old woman alone for the present, and when our more important affairs are brought to an end it will be quite time enough for you to think of pulling down the cottage of Dame Dagley about her ears."

"Give me no more of your advice, Arnheim," retorted the young man, "for I am resolved to revenge myself for the mischief she has tried to do me, and never shall I know rest till my purpose has been fully accomplished."

"Humph! you had better by half have accepted the challenge I just now gave you."

"None but a madman would accept the challenge of an idiot in his cups," answered Henry Neville. "Lie down and sleep, and to-morrow, when you become sober, you will be ashamed of the folly you have this night been guilty of."

These words were uttered in a tone of contempt, and as the young man left the room, Arnheim sprang from his seat and rushed furiously after him. At that moment Nicodemus Dove happened to enter the room, and intently engaged in the perusal of one of his own poems, he saw not the danger with which he was threatened till he found himself in the grasp of the enraged German. Observing, however, the fierce glances of the foreigner, he fell upon his knees, exclaiming in accents of the most abject terror,—

"Oh, mercy! mercy! good Mr. Stranger, and don't look so fiercely upon a poor unfortunate poet, who would sooner have gone a mile out of his way than venture into the presence of such a cut-throat looking stranger."

"Derfiend! what do you mean by cut-throat?"

"Nothing offensive, my good sir, I assure you," answered Nicodemus; "I only meant to say that you are a soldier, and you know, all gentlemen of your profession have a knack of spilling blood that is not agreeable to persons of a literary turn like myself."

"Humph! so you are a poet?"

"I have that honour," answered the other, "and if you will only promise not to injure me, I'll write you verses for nothing as long as I live."

"What is your name?"

"Nicodemus Dove."

"Do you do nothing else but write poetry?"

"That's all I can assure you, sir, and I flatter myself that my verses are well worth your hearing."

"You may spare yourself the trouble of repeating them," exclaimed Arnheim; "for, to speak my mind, I never had any great liking for that sort of rubbise. However, as you seem to be a mere simpleton you may go, for when first we met I thought you had been that villain who just now left me with a taunt upon his lips."

"I see—you thought Master Henry Neville had returned."

"I did—and seized you by the throat in mistake for him."

"And a very pretty mistake you had like to have made of it," exclaimed the other, "for the world would have lost a poet had you strangled me, and then——"

"Silence this idle prate, for I am in no humour to bear with your folly," exclaimed Arnheim. "Leave me, sirrah! and of all things take care never to enter my presence again."

"Depend upon it I'll take your advice," replied the other, "for the commencement of our acquaintance is quite sufficient to convince me that we are not destined to become friends. I have told you I am Nicodemus Dove, and the Doves for many generations past have been remarkable for their gentleness and peacefulness of their habits."

"And for their folly as well, if I may judge from the precious specimen before me. But you have not yet told me, sirrah, what business brought you here?"

"The truth is, I didn't come on any particular business," answered the other. "I was occupied in reading my last piece of poetry, and was so lost in its beauties, that I directed my steps towards this chamber without being aware of where I was going. By-the-by, sir, shall I read some of it? you'll be delighted with the sublimity of the ideas and the interest of its plot."

"Bah! go to the devil with you."

"Thank you, sir," cried Dove, "but I begin to believe that I'm in that gentleman's company already."

"Eh!" exclaimed the choleric German, "what's that you are muttering, sirrah?"

"I was merely observing," replied the poet, "that I hoped I was in company with a gentleman. But come, you seem out of sorts, so I'll put you into good humour by reading a few lines from the last inspiration of my muse.

"No, no," exclaimed Arnheim; "I don't want to have anything to do with your lines; they put me too much in mind of what you English people call the gallows."

"Ah!" replied Nicodemus Dove, "and my lines happen to be upon a very exalted subject. They are addressed to the stars, and commence in the following impressive manner,—

> "Ye pretty twinklers, that shine so bright,
> And look so brightly on a frosty night,
> Look down on me who thus your praises sing,
> And—"

"Enough of this rubbish," interrupted Captain Arnheim; "this is poetry run mad, and rather would I drink off a glass of salt and water than sit here to listen to another of your execrable rhymes. Here is wine for you, man, and when you have imbibed about half a bottle, I should like to ask you a few questions?"

Nicodemus Dove had no objection whatever to the wine, and having swallowed three or four glasses of it, the awe which had been inspired by the blustering of the foreigner began to subside, and he expressed his perfect readiness to enter into any subject upon which his companion desired to speak.

"In the first place, then," said Arnheim, "I would know how long you have been acquainted with this family?"

"Ever since I was a child."

"Do you live with Sir Richard Langdale, or are you only here on a visit?"

"I'm on a visit," replied Nicodemus, in a simpering tone; "there's an attraction here, sir, that I can't resist, and perhaps some day or another I may carry off the prize, though between ourselves there's plenty more on the very same suit."

"Ah! a little love affair, I suppose."

"Exactly so; the beauty of Sir Richard Langdale's daughters is not to be resisted by one so ardent as myself, and to tell you the truth, I have some hopes of becoming one of the family before long."

"Indeed! and pray which of the young ladies has the honour of obtaining your preference?"

"That's more than I can tell you," answered Nicodemus Dove, "for I'm placed in rather a perplexing situation, seeing that both the girls have an equal share of my love."

"But the law won't allow you to marry them both."

"I know it, and for that very reason I've been trying for some time past to make up my mind which to have. Blanche would perhaps be my choice if there was no obstacle in the way, but she has two lovers already, and as they are both men of mettle, I've been thinking the wisest course I can take will be to pay respects to Catherine Langdale."

"Does the young lady give any encouragement to your addresses?"

"I can't say that she's very fond of me yet," answered Nicodemus Dove, "but time works wonders, and I've good hopes that by-and-by she'll yield to the soft persuasions of poetry. I've written sonnets out of number to her beauty, and where is the female heart that can resist flattery when broadside after broadside is poured upon her ?"

"Ay; but she may chance to have another lover."

"I don't care if she has a score of them, so that I get the good-will of her father. Sir Richard is a man of discrimination, and he'll not be unmindful of the honour of having a poet in his family."

"Nay, if he has sense, he'll take care to prevent his daughter marrying a fool."

"Mr. Foreigner!" exclaimed Nicodemus, "I have not the honour of knowing your name, but I must beg leave to remind you that your language is beginning to grow offensive. The aspirations of my genius have been given to the world, and no one till the present moment has ever called me a fool."

"That," replied Arnheim, "is because no one has taken the trouble to read what you call the aspirations of your genius. I have been compelled to hear some wretched doggrel, that you call poetry, and judging from the sample, I think you would prove yourself a wiser man if you would stick to plain prose in future. Sir Richard is a straight forward man, and will not, I should think, give his daughter to a fellow that utters nonsense every time he opens his mouth."

"But suppose Sir Richard Langdale is so far in my power that he dare not refuse me."

"In your power ?"

"Ay; he wouldn't like to be sent to the scaffold."

"He has not done anything to deserve it."

"Hasn't he though? so it's nothing to conspire against the Queen of England."

"Who, besides yourself, dare say that he has done so?" demanded Arnheim. "The character of the baronet stands high, yet is it to be blasted by the scandalous reports of an insignificent fellow like yourself?"

"You may call me what names you please," exclaimed the other, "but I know all about the treason, and what's more I've pretty good reason to believe that you and the priest are mixed up with it."

"Ha!" vociferated Arnheim, "have you so little care for your life that you must needs tempt me to take it away?"

"Oh, you won't do that for your own sake," returned Nicodemus, "and as for myself, I don't mean to give a hint of the affair that has come to my knowledge, because if I did, there would be an end of my hopes of marriage in their family. Besides, Sir Richard Langdale and I are on good terms, and it's hardly likely that I should send to the scaffold the father of the two girls I am in love with."

"Fool! cannot you fix your choice on one of them ?"

"I suppose I must do so by-and-by," answered Nicodemus Dove 'and yet it is harder to make the choice than you seem to imagine. Blanche is the one I most admire, but the girl is proud, and turns a deaf ear to me, even when I express my passion in the language of poetry."

"Besides which it appears the old man is determined that she shall be the wife of Henry Neville."

"And the girl is equally determined not to marry any other than the man of her choice."

"Psha! what will be the use of resistance against the commands of her father ?"

"Why," replied Nicodemus Dove, "you ought to know as well as I do, that when womankind make up their minds to anything, it aint easy to turn them from it. Perhaps Blanche happens to know that young Neville is in the conspiracy against the government, and if so she must be well aware of what his fate will be if he should happen to be discovered."

"Nonsense man!" exclaimed the German, "there's no foundation for the foolish notion of a conspiracy."

"So much the better," answered Nicodemus, "for I esteem my friend, the baronet, and should be sorry if he got himself into a scrape through joining in a treasonable plot. The subject would be too tempting a one to resist, but it would be a melancholy task to sit down and write an elegy upon the tragical death of Sir Richard Langdale for the part he had taken in the wicked conspiracy against our sovereign lady the queen."

"You seem to have made up your mind, then, that there is a conspiracy?"

"I'm quite certain there is."

"And to speak the truth, I have heard something of it before now," answered Arnheim. "The queen, I believe, is not liked by a good many of her subjects on account of her favouring the Protestant religion, and those who adhere to the old form of worship have resolved to bestow the crown upon some one of their own creed. Such a plot, I believe, is going on, but you must not imagine that either Sir Richard, or we who have the honour to call ourselves his friends, have any thing to do with it."

"Well," exclaimed the other, "I hope it's as you say, but I can't help thinking that Sir Richard Langdale, who is a Papist, has something more to do with it than he would like to be known to people that are not of his own way of thinking."

"If such is your opinion," exclaimed Arnheim, "be careful how you give a hint of it to any other person. Depend upon it, Master Dove, I shall keep a watchful eye upon you, and the moment you open your lips to say a word against any one of us will be nearly the last you will spend in this world."

"Why you don't mean to say you would murder me?"

"You cannot misunderstand what I have said," replied Arnheim, "and I shall therefore leave you to reflect on the danger of speaking about things that don't concern you will bring upon yourself. Be wise, therefore, or there will be one poet the less to scribble the nonsense that comes into his head."

"Nonsense!" exclaimed Dove, indignantly; "if you would only listen to the remainder of the poem I began to read to you upon the stars, you would soon confess that the ideas contained in it are beautiful!"

"Psha! I have already heard too much of the rubbish."

"You are a Goth to call it rubbish," exclaimed the other. "I wonder where you'll find your beauties of language then? Certainly not in that thick skull of yours."

"Ha," exclaimed Arnheim, "you would insult me, would you? Now I was going to ask you to take another cup of wine with me, but I'll revenge myself by drinking every drop of it myself;" and suiting the action to the word, he drank off in succession three or four draughts of the luscious beverage, so that in a few minutes he began to show evident symptoms of the effect it had upon his brain.

"Now listen to me, Mr. Poet," he exclaimed, looking fiercely at his alarmed auditor, "and take a hint from the caution I am going to give you. You have talked about treasons that are supposed to be going on, and all sorts of other strange fancies, but you had better mind what you are about, because you've got people to deal with who know how to revenge themselves when they know that they have got an enemy to contend against. I shall keep my eye upon you, and upon the least suspicion that you mean to play us false, I shall take the affair into my own hands. So now I have spoken my mind pretty freely, and if you would keep your bones whole in your skin, run off as quickly as ever your legs will carry you!"

"There's one advantage I have," answered Nicodemus, "for if I run I'm sure you can't follow me, except at the risk of a fall,—

"So now, old chap, we'll try it man to man,—
I'm off—and you may catch me if you can."

And with this splendid effusion, Nicodemus Dove made a rapid retreat from the room.

CHAPTER VIII.

I will revenge all former injuries—
Cancel the debt that is between us,
And when my purposes are all complete,
Wed the fair maid whose scornful pride hath
Urged her to reject me.—THE ITALIAN.

IT was on the same evening to which the incidents of the last chapter belong, that the Outlaw betook himself to the cottage of the Dagleys, to confer with those whom he had good reson to believe were faithful in his cause. His present visit, however, was more particularly to the dame, who, in compliance with his wish, accompanied him to the outside of the house, where they might speak together without being overheard.

"I have reason to believe," he said, "that an attack is this night meditated upon your family, and my object in coming hither is to assure you that in the event of my suspicions being realised, I have made preparations for your defence. In fact, a party of the foresters are now within a few hundred yards of this spot, and should there be occasion, they will immediately advance for the protection of your family."

"We need no protection," answered the dame, "for our poverty alone is sufficient to render it impossible that any one will seek to molest us."

"Have you, then, so soon forgotten the threat of Henry Neville?"

"They were words uttered in the heat of anger, and, my life for it, had no meaning in them."

"They had more meaning in them than you think for," he replied, "and a brief period will serve to prove that I do not unnecessarily seek to excite your alarm. The man I speak of is vindictive, and terrible in his anger; your have excited his wrath, and never will he rest contented till you have felt the full weight of his indignation."

"Have I then angered him by once or twice thwarting his designs against you?"

"You have."

"Be it so," she replied; "there are, at least, laws for the poor as well as the rich, and if he commits violence against them he will suffer the consequences."

"Perhaps so," exclaimed the Outlaw, "but you would not live to witness his punishment."

"And if he kills me," answered the old woman, "it would be but abridging my days by a brief period."

"But I have received favours and kindness from you," exclaimed the fugitive; "and it therefore becomes my solemn duty to guard you against the evil machinations of an insidious enemy. Henry Neville will come here to-night to seek me, and when he finds not his enemy, he will wreak his vengeance upon those who have foiled him in his designs."

"Are you sure that he intends coming here?"

"There is every reason to believe he does."

"Then will he meet with a warmer reception than he expects," returned Dame Dagley. "My husband and my son, by good fortune, are both at home, and we have arms enough in the house to serve us in case of need. Nay, I myself can wield a weapon with the best of them, when there is need of it, and our enemies would meet with so stout a resistance, that I much doubt whether they would ever wish to repeat their visit."

"You forget, dame," replied the Outlaw, "that Neville would not come without sufficient force to render his designs almost certain. He has all the retainers of Sir Richard Langdale at his beck and call, and I have heard you say that there is no kindly feeling between your family and the tenants of the baronet's."

"It must be confessed that there is an old grudge between us," she replied,

" for they like not that my son and husband should now and then kill a deer belonging to Sir Richard, and to please their master, they have all arrayed themselves against us. But our cottage is our castle, and if any attempt is made to carry it by storm, the besiegers will return home to their master with but a sorry account of their expedition."

" That," answered the Outlaw, " will depend upon the number of men Henry Neville brings with him. I suspect he means to come well prepared to meet a sturdy resistance, and in that expectation I have a body of foresters in ambush, who, on the first sound of tumult, will hasten hither to your assistance. With their assistance we may hope to turn the tide in your favour, and after a severe defeat it may be expected the enemy will be in no hurry to repeat their attack."

" But after all, these fears of yours may be groundless."

" They may," he replied; " but even if that should be the case, it is well to be prepared for the worst. Neville would hear, perhaps, of the preparations made to thwart his designs, and it would serve as a lesson for him in future, not to molest those who have not done him an injury either by word or thought."

" I am grateful for the interest you have taken in us," exclaimed Dame Dagley; " but I'm afraid there is more real danger to yourself than to us. Should Henry Neville come and find you here, he would not miss the opportunity of making you his prisoner, even though it could only be done by the sacrifice of a score or two of lives."

" Be assured, dame," returned the Outlaw, " he will not find it an easy task to get me in his power. I have told you there is plenty of assistance at hand, and as I believe the men will prove true to me, he will find his projects fail, even at the time when he is most in expectation of success. However, I will not slight your advice, but retire a short distance from this spot, and there lie in wait till I see that there is a necessity for coming to your rescue; and even then, I shall not bring my followers with me, unless it should appear that there is no other way left by which to defeat the purposes of the enemy."

He then turned away, and Dame Dagley having watched him as long as his retiring form was visible, gave expression to her joy at the probability of his being beyond the reach of danger.

" Thank Heaven, he is now safe!" she at length exclaimed; " yet on me and mine, I doubt not they will pour the full tide of their wrath. And so let them. I have suffered much, but I can yet endure more when it is in a good cause; for, Outlaw as he is, he has ever shown a nobler heart than those who, under the pretence of justice, would hunt him to death. I have been the means of saving him from the arm of the ruthless Henry Neville, and I will yet do my best to preserve him, even though it should give me over to the vengeance of his enemies."

During the utterance of the last few words, she moved towards the cottage, the door of which she was about to enter, when her arm was firmly grasped by Henry Neville, who, in a suppressed tone of malice, exclaimed in her ear :—

" Now, devil's dame!—where is the villain thou wert mad enough to rescue from my vengeance;—tell me, without delay, where I may find him, or by my soul I'll wrench from thee the truth."

" Thy soul!" she exclaimed, with bitter emphasis—" thy soul, Henry Neville, is withered and lost!—Get thee hence, I say, for I know nothing of him thou askest for !"

" I will soon make thee confess, thou accursed witch," vociferated the other,— " nay, I will find his retreat, even though thou dost hoard the secret in thy heart of hearts !"

" Pluck it out then!" exclaimed the dame, undaunted by the violence by which she had been assailed; " pluck it out, I say, for thou shalt not know from me, unless thou canst get it so. Murder me, if thou wilt—murder me, I say, for I scorn thy puny anger, even as I scorn thyself. A poor, miserable, abject woman scorns a high born noble like thee, and puts thee to shame."

" Thou liest, woman, when thou sayst thou hast no knowledge of my enemy's retreat."

" I confess the lie," she replied; " I know well enough, man, where the fugitive is lurking; I could find him for thee at murk midnight; but he is safe for anything that old Dame Dagley will say to his injury."

"Curse thee for a black, thrice-sold witch!" exclaimed Henry Neville, furiously. "Thou has favoured my enemy, and for that thou shalt not escape thy doom though thou hast been lucky enough to avoid fire and faggot."

"Psha!" she replied, coldly, "thy words pass by me as the idle wind."

Thou dost not know me, woman," exclaimed Neville, unable to curb his wrath; "thou dost not know me, I say, or thou wouldst not thus have tempted my fury."

"I would, I have done so," answered the old woman; "I know thee for what thou art, but yet I feared thee not. I am prepared for all thy black heart may prompt thee to do, and am ready to die rather than reveal the secret thou hast the baseness to attempt to wring from me."

"Hark you, Dame Dagley," exclaimed Henry Neville, "I would not pollute my hands with thy blood, for it is even baser than the foul water that remains stagnant in yonder ditch-puddle. I have, moreover, reasons of my own for wishing thee to live, but, as I have life and strength, and as I may die unshriven and unabsolved

No. 8.

of sin, I will give thee but one minute more to answer the question I have put to thee. Where is the villain who, but for thy vile plotting, would ere now have been in the hands of his enemy?"

"Henry Neville," she replied, tauntingly, "the man you seek was not long since in your power. You had a weapon in your hand, why did you not slay him?"

"Ha!" he exclaimed, stung by her words, and the tone in which they were uttered; "the taunt thou hast uttered to insult me, has sealed thy fate?"

Whilst yet speaking, he suddenly sprang towards the old woman, and seizing her by the throat, was about to strangle her, when Martha Dagley, who had been for some little time watching them from the door, rushed forward, and exclaimed, as she presented a loaded pistol at Henry Neville,—

"Villain! forbear, I command you! quit your tiger's grasp upon my mother, or as Heaven is my witness, thou hast not another minute's life left in thee!"

"Ha! is it thou, my pretty wench?" he cried, as he instantly relaxed his grasp. "Come hither, Patty—approach me, girl—nay, I pledge thee my solemn word I will not harm thee."

"I will not trust to thy solemn promise," she replied.

"Why art thou here then?"

"To save my mother from the cowardly violence of a ruffian," she replied. "But I wish not to speak to thee, Henry Neville, let my mother and myself pass without interruption into our cottage, or, woman as I am, I will lay thee at my feet a bleeding corse."

"Psha!" he exclaimed, with pretended kindness, "it is madness to oppose yourself against me in this way; I have asked to be informed where the Outlaw has sought concealment, and you threaten me with death."

"Ay," replied Martha Dagley, "and armed as I am, it is in my power to fulfil the threat I have uttered."

"Surely, you do not wish to murder me?"

"It is my nature to shrink with horror from the sight of blood," she replied, "but, in defence of my mother, there is no act of violence that I dare not commit. Once more, therefore, I demand, will you allow my mother and myself to pass into our own cottage without hinderance or molestation?"

"Why, ay," answered Henry Neville, "since chance has given you an advantage over me, I must needs yield to your demand. But remember, girl, the insult I have this night received, will not pass unavenged. You will yet have reason to repent the rash step you have taken, though the moment for the execution of my purpose will come upon you without warning or notice. You are both free to enter the cottage, and I promise not to molest you—at least for the present!"

"Your threats, young man, we heed not," exclaimed Dame Dagley; "for knowing the enemy we have to deal with, we shall always be prepared for any act of villany that he may design against us. So now, farewell to you, Master Henry Neville, and if you would not waste your time, lose none of it to-night in a vain search after the Outlaw."

The two females then entered the cottage, whilst Neville stood watching them, and gnashing his teeth at the utter defeat which he had just sustained through them; at length, as the door closed, he exclaimed, in a voice husky with anger,—

"May my heaviest curses light upon yonder obstinate woman! Their refusal to point out the lurking place of this Outlaw has baffled all the hopes that induced me to visit this spot at an hour like this. But I will yet be revenged—fully and most amply revenged for all the insults and disappointments I have endured since my arrival in this neighbourhood!"

He now stood listening in breathless silence, for distant sounds fell upon his ear, and as the footsteps approached, he became the more anxious to ascertain whether those who were coming were friends or foes. At length several persons emerged from a thicket at no great distance off, and in an instant all his suspense and anxiety had vanished.

"By all my hopes," he exclaimed aloud, "it is Arnheim, with some of the retainers of Sir Richard Langdale, who come this way. Now, then, thou black and hateful hag,—*now* thou shalt feel the vengeance I can hurl upon thee! Thou art in my power, and by Heaven I will not leave this place till all within yonder cottage have been buried in one common ruin!"

"Why, Harry, my boy," exclaimed the German, as he approached, "what has happened since we last saw each other? you look as grave and melancholy as an owl to-night, and your face tells me a tale that you have not been best pleased with the company you have found in this queer-looking neighbourhood."

"The truth is," replied Henry Neville, "that I have been foiled, defeated in my views—and that too by a woman."

"More shame for you, Harry; but who and where is the woman that has had the honour of outwitting you?"

"She and her mother are now in yonder cottage," answered the other, pointing towards the place.

"Indeed!—why, if I mistake not, it is Dagley's house, where I and Father Francis found shelter till it was safe for us to make our appearance at the castle."

"It is," answered Henry Neville, "and I have strong suspicions that the Outlaw is concealed there by these Dagleys."

"Then let us summon them all to surrender at discretion."

"It would be useless to do so, for the men are armed, and have the advantage of fighting under cover."

"At least," observed Captain Arnheim, "there can be no harm in our asking for admittance."

"Nay," replied Neville, "I tell you it would be useless, for I just now heard them barricade the door, and though numerous enough to make an attack, we are all set at defiance."

"D——n!—then if no other way is left for us, we must make our way through the window."

And without waiting to hear what reply was made to this, he darted his sword through the casement, and was about to make his way through the breach he had formed when Stephen Dagley presented himself at the place to prevent his admission. The German, however, was not to be easily foiled, and as he still persisted in his attempt, Stephen discharged the carbine with which he had armed himself at the moment when the crash of broken glass warned him that an attack was about to be commenced on the cottage.

"Pho!" cried Captain Arnheim, "dog that thou art, thou hast, luckily for me, shot wide of thy mark. Join me in the attack, Harry Neville, for the war has commenced in earnest, and it is time for us to show that we are not to be driven off by the report of a little gunpowder. Fire your pistol into the thatch, my boy, and burn the vermin out of their nests."

Neville needed no second bidding to do mischief, and discharging his weapon as he had been directed, a fierce assault was commenced, which was as fiercely resisted by those within the place. At length, however, flames began to burst forth from the roof, which quickly spreading to other parts of the cottage, the unfortunate inmates were compelled to seek their preservation from a horrible death. Immediately afterwards the door was thrown open, and Stephen Dagley came forth carrying his wife in his arms; Martin closely followed him with his almost fainting sister, and as each of them quitted the cottage they were made prisoners by their inexorable enemies. The fresh air speedily revived Dame Dagley, who, gazing round upon the scene of destruction, seemed to feel with terrible force the helpless situation to which the last few minutes had reduced them.

"Monsters!" she exclaimed, "whither would you now drag us? If to death, why not slay us on this spot where you have rendered us homeless and beggars."

"Ha, dame!" cried Henry Neville, with fiendish triumph, "said I not just now that you should soon be made to feel the full weight of my vengeance, and have I not most *honourably* kept my promise? Your cottage is levelled to the dust, and you, with kith and kin, are in the power of the very man you lately affected to despise. Hag of darkness! you it was who arrested my steel when I was about to bury it in the heart of the felon Outlaw; for that act of yours I swore to be revenged, and *I am* !"

"Have mercy, I implore you," cried the old woman, broken in spirit by the misfortunes that had overwhelmed them, "suffer but my husband and my children to go free, and I will follow even to death without a murmur! Deny me this—and my curses shall cling to you for ever."

But she spoke to one who was deaf to every appeal for mercy, and looking at her with an expressson of concentrated hate, he turned away, and addressing himself to the retainers, exclaimed,—

"We have no time to lose in this place; forward, my lads,—forward, and conduct your prisoners with all speed to the castle of Holmwood."

"Ay, forward, by all means!" added Captain Arnheim, who was evidently apprehensive of danger, and scarcely had the words been uttered, than the Outlaw, accompanied by a number of woodmen, suddenly made his appearance in that part through which lay their route to Holmwood. All of them were well armed, and from their number it might be inferred, that in the event of a skirmish the fortune of war would most certainly decide in their favour.

"Hold!" exclaimed the Outlaw, seeing it was their purpose to persist in advancing; "approach not another step for your lives!" then addressing himself to those about him, he added,—

"My friends, do some of you remain to maintain this place against the enemy, while the rest follow me to the rescue of our captive friends."

As he approached Henry Neville gave hasty orders to one of Sir Richard's retainers.

"Haste, Gabriel," he whispered, "and bring hither without delay, the remainder of our men. Speed, man, speed, or they will scarce be in time to save us from falling into the hands of the enemy."

Thus adjured by his superior, the person who had received these orders hastened away in the direction of the castle, and the Outlaw then addressing himself to his haughty rival, said,—

"Henry Neville, it is now my turn to triumph; for overpowered as you are by numbers, resistance would only lead to the slaughter of half these man."

"For the present you triumph," answered the other sullenly, "but the advantage you boast of will last only till the arrival of more of our friends who will hasten here immediately after they learn from my messenger the situation in which we are placed."

"Expect nothing from the assistance of your friend," exclaimed the Outlaw, "for the man you have sent to apprise them of your danger will find the road to the castle occupied by men belonging to our party. The bridge is destroyed—your retreat cut off, and your only alternative is to yield to a fate that is not to be averted."

"The man knows the country well," answered Henry Neville, "and he has only to make his way to the next bridge, which leads to Holmwood Castle, though by a more circuitous route."

"Which will make the assistance he brings too late," returned the other; "all these things have been carefully weighed in my mind, and in order to prevent a rescue, it is my intention to convey you instantly from this place."

"Villain!" cried Neville, furious at the danger in which he had fallen; "whither would you convey us?"

"To the Outlaw's Hall."

"Where is that?"

"Beneath my own favourite tree in the greenwood. You sought me, Henry Neville, and have found me, though not quite so unprepared as was expected. We meet, but not in friendship, and will not part till we have settled all the differences that our rivalry in love has occasioned."

"Again I caution you not to boast too soon," exclaimed Neville, "for the triumph you at present exult in will be of short duration."

"What hope have you of escape?"

"I rely upon the good fortune that always attends me," replied the young man. "Do you think, sirrah, so little of my generalship as to imagine that all my resources are gone on the first failure; or that I should blindly suffer myself to fall nto the hands of those from whom I have neither pity nor mercy to expect? True, I am now in your power, but presently the tables will be turned, and then it will be for me to exult in the capture of my enemy."

"You cannot then imagine it possible that all your good fortune has deserted you at once?"

"No, by Heaven, I cannot! a few moments of captivity will be all the inconvenience I shall endure, whilst thou, in thine own turn, art doomed to become the prisoner of a man from whom thou hast neither favour nor mercy to expect."

Captain Arnheim could not patiently endure the unexpected reverse that had occurred to them, and even after all the rest had submitted themselves prisoners, he made use of the most violent efforts to release himself from those into whose hands he had fallen. All the attempts however that he made proved absortive, and at length giving way to his ungovernable rage he exclaimed:—

"Fiends and devils! hell I believe has broke loose in this forest, or we should not have been deserted at such a time as this. Yonder witch hath palsied our arms, and made women of us all, when most there was need to fight for our lives and liberty. Unhand me, dogs that ye are—unhand me, I say, for I'll not fall without one blow in behalf of myself and friends."

And so saying he suddenly broke away from them, and snatching an axe from the nearest woodman, threw himself into an attitude of the most determined resistance.

"Off, villains!" he hoarsely exclaimed; "stir not, on your lives, for I will strike the first man that approaches me lifeless to the earth!"

"Madman!" interposed the Outlaw, "suspend this useless violence, for your single arm can effect no good service against the numbers by whom you are surrounded!"

"You at least shall not live to triumph over the men who came forth to capture you," exclaimed the German, and, poising the axe above his head, he was about to strike down the Outlaw, when the formidable weapon was suddenly wrenched from his grasp. At the same moment he was again seized, and his arms so confined as to prevent all fear of his being able to commit any further mischief.

"D——n!" he growled, "everything seems to be going against us to-day!"

"You would have slain me," observed the Outlaw, calmly, "and even had your design been successful, of what advantage would my death have been to you?"

"I should at least have had the satisfaction of slaying the man I call my enemy."

"The satisfaction would have been a very brief one," replied the Outlaw, "for, had I fallen, my friends here would have revenged my death upon the instant."

"Doubtless the fellows would soon have butchered me," exclaimed Captain Arnheim, "but, at all events, *you*, as well myself, would have been sent to your long account. Besides, I should have served my friend, Henry Neville, who would then have had no rival to deprive him of the love of her he would make his wife."

"That is a matter which we cannot argue at this time or in this place," returned the Outlaw, "so come, prepare ye to march with us to our greenwood tree."

Preparations were now made to proceed without delay to the place he had spoken of, but, ere the march could be commenced, a bugle note was heard at no great distance off, announcing the approach of another body of men. Henry Neville instantly recognised the signal, and, releasing his arm for a moment, he answered the sound by three or four notes on the bugle with which he had taken the precaution to provide himself.

"Now," he exclaimed, addressing himself in triumph to the Outlaw, "your idle boasting has no sooner been uttered than your supposed advantage is lost. The blast you just now heard on my bugle will guide our friends to the place where you hold us in captivity. Outlaw, your good fortune forsakes you; it is now time that you look to yourself."

He had scarcely uttered these words than a large party of Sir Richard Langdale's armed retainers came marching in compact order towards them. At their approach the woodsmen, who seemed to be stricken with sudden terror, threw down their arms, and commenced a precipitous retreat, leaving the Outlaw to the certainty of falling into the hands of the enemy. In a few moments both he and the Dagleys were seized, and precautions taken to prevent the possibility of escape. The triumph of Henry Neville was thus rendered complete, and, striding up to the fugitive, he exclaimed, in all the fulness of his gratification,—

"How now, sir of the greenwood, are not the tables already turned, as I told you they would be? Your majesty of the forest must now with me, for there is no hope that the knaves you trusted will return to your rescue."

"I yield myself to my fate," answered the Outlaw, with calm dignity of demeanour, "and whatever may be my doom, you shall at least be forced to confess that I endure it with firmness and courage."

"You acknowledge yourself vanquished?"

"Why, yes," he replied, "the rank cowardice of the men I placed my trust in has indeed given you the advantage over me. Lead me where you will—do with me as you please—even though torture and an excruciating death be my doom. Onwards, sir! I follow with all submission."

"We shall see how far a rigorous imprisonment may serve to bring down your haughty spirit," exclaimed the other. "At any rate, there is now an end of any hopes you may have entertained of making Blanche Langdale your wife; you will, in your gloomy cell, reflect upon the impossibility of her ever being yours, and perhaps, on condition that you give up all future claim to her hand, I may be induced to intercede with Sir Richard for your liberation from his dungeon."

"I neither ask, nor will I receive any favour from you," replied the Outlaw, haughtily. "Blanche Langdale has been pleased to bestow upon me her warmest affection, and I should be a black-hearted villain were I to surrender her over to a man whom I know she hates and despises."

"Never fear; but her hate will all turn to love when there is no longer a rival in my way," exclaimed Neville. "Besides, I have her father's sanction to the marriage, and however averse she may be to accept me for her husband, she will be compelled to accompany me to the altar."

"And you would wed the girl even under such dishonourable circumstances as you speak of?"

"To be sure I will—I have resolved to make Blanche Langdale my wife, and even her hatred and contempt shall not serve to turn me from my purpose."

Dame Dagley, who had hitherto been a silent listener to all that was going on, now advanced between the two men who had charge of her, and addressing Henry Neville in a tone of prophecy, she said,—

"You little know, young man, the misery and despair that you are bringing upon yourself;—the treason you are plotting will soon be discovered, and the punishment that follows such crimes you know as well as I do. The axe and the block must be your doom, and then will come the triumph of those you would now crush beneath your feet."

"Speak lower," he exclaimed, "or my dagger shall at once deprive you of all chance of your expected triumph. These men know not of the plot you speak of, and the first word you utter to betray my secret will consign you and your fellow-prisoner to instant death!"

"Moderate your violence, young man," she replied, tauntingly, "or you will be your own betrayer to these retainers of Sir Richard Langdale. So far your secret is safe with me; but if violence should be resorted to against yonder Outlaw, I shall not for another moment hesitate to declare the purpose of your present visit to this part of the country."

"How have you become possessed of this secret?" he demanded, as he drew her a little apart.

"Through the thoughtlessness or folly of your own confederates," she replied.

"What! the strangers who have recently arrived?"

"Even so."

"Have they been fools enough to make you their confidant?"

"No," answered the old woman;" but I overheard them during one of their conferences, and though they spoke in dark hints, I could yet make out quite enough to convince me that there was a plot brewing for the overthrow of the queen and government. They are both of them foreigners, and are willing to aid you in deposing our good sovereign for the sake of restoring the old religion."

"Are they aware that you heard their conversation?"

"They knew not of my being so near," she replied, "and fearing their violence, I crept away without being discovered, as soon as I had gathered sufficient for my purpose."

"And what bribe do you require to keep your secret?"

"Neither your gold nor your favour," she replied.

"You have at least cause to dread my vengeance, should it appear that your death is necessary for my own safety."

"I have lived too long in the world to be afraid of death," answered the old woman; " and whatever violence you may think proper to commit, I have at least the consolation of knowing that it would only hurry on the fate you are anxious to avoid. You can murder me, Henry Neville, but life will not depart from me so suddenly that I shall not have time to declare the crime meditated by you and your associates."

"What's the matter with you, Harry?" exclaimed the German, who now approached them.

"Nothing," he replied; "except that the old woman has been pleading hard for the liberty of her friend, the Outlaw."

"And is that the only reason for your looking so black and angry?"

"That's all," answered Neville; " and even if it were not, I am in no humour just now to enter into an explanation that you have no right to demand."

"Humph! do you want to pick a quarrel with me?"

"I seek not to quarrel with any man," replied Neville, "much less with one that I would fain regard as my friend. Suffice it to know that this hag hath moved me to anger; but the occasion of it must be explained at some future time."

"May I venture to ask what you mean to do with the prisoners?"

"They will be conveyed instantly to Holmwood Castle."

"There, I suppose, to be kept in close confinement?"

"Ay, there are dungeons strong enough to hold them."

"But what will be said if it becomes known that Sir Richard Langdale holds some of the queen's subjects in captivity?"

"Sir Richard possesses the authority to imprison all suspicious characters, and to try them in a court of which he is supreme judge."

"How! has he the power of life and death over his fellow subjects?"

"I am not quite certain that he would go so far as to send a man to the gibbet," answered Henry Neville, "but such a power has been in the hands of his ancestors for several generations. The privilege was, I believe, bestowed upon a former member of the family for some great service that he performed for the crown."

The Outlaw had by this time approached pretty near to the spot where they were standing, and having heard the latter part of their conversation, he muttered, loud enough to be heard,—

"Sir Richard Langdale possesses such a power as you speak of, but in the present instance it would be too dangerous an exercise of authority to put into practice."

"Where would be the danger?" asked Neville, haughtily.

"The question must come from his own lips ere I answer it," replied the Outlaw, in an equally frigid tone.

" Perhaps he may not take the trouble, since you are a prisoner in his hands, and may be sent to speedy execution."

" He will do well to pause ere he attempt it," exclaimed the Outlaw, "for there will be those left behind who would not suffer their kinsman to perish by an ignominious death without hurling a terrible retribution against the man who, in pursuance of his own feelings of revenge, had brought shame and dishonour on one of their own family."

" Indeed !" cried Henry Neville ; " I should have imagined that the Outlaw had, by his own acts, brought down upon them all the disgrace of which you would make us believe we stand in so much fear."

" Those who know me," answered the other, "are aware the charges brought against me by my enemies are the wicked inventions of those who seek my ruin."

" That is an excuse easily made," answered Neville, " but the very fact of your so anxiously concealing your name proves, that the charges are not so false as you represent."

" Am I then expected to reveal myself to those whom I despise ?"

" Why, it would have been the wiser course considering the chance it might have afforded you of getting out of the very unpleasant dilemma you have fallen into."

"My own misfortunes I can endure without a murmur," replied the Outlaw, " but I will not bring shame upon those whose honour I hold dearer than my own. Sir Richard Langdale may, for the gratification of his own private revenge, adjudge me to death, yet not even the fear of an ignominious doom shall force from me a confession of who I am."

" And yet, observed Henry Neville, " you can scarcely hope that the secret can be kept for any long time."

" Humph ! 'tis a paltry spirit that can triumph over the fall even of an enemy.

" I exult," replied the other, " because in your fall I see my own safety. You are possessed of a secret upon which my life depends, and when once my enemy is removed, I may hope to see our plot proceed without fear of discovery."

" Are you quite sure," demanded the Outlaw, " that your proceedings are not watched by some of the agents of the government ?"

" There can be little fear of that," answered Henry Neville, " since a plot like this would be checked the instant it became known to those who are interested in preventing the danger with which their sovereign is threatened. But perhaps you have yourself given information in the hope that a timely warning to the queen will be the means of securing your own pardon."

" No—by Heaven, I have not !" exclaimed the Outlaw. " It was my duty to have done so I admit, but, despising as I do the character of a spy, I contented myself with the thought that it was in my power to avert your evil designs whenever I saw that my longer silence would be culpable."

" And now, instead of being able to denounce us, you are a prisoner in the hands of your deadliest foes."

" Why, ay," replied the Outlaw, " the base cowardice of those I depended on has given you an advantage over me. But enough of this—lead me where you will—do with me as you please ; for I can endure all your malice even though torture and death may be my doom. Lead the way, Henry Neville—your prisoner will follow with all submission to his fate."

" By Jove ! that's sensibly said," exclaimed the other, and then addressing the retainers, he continued,—" Now, sirrahs, let us commence our march towards Holmwood Castle, and, as you value your lives, see that the prisoners escape not."

In a few minutes the necessary arrangements were completed, and, headed by Henry Neville and the German, they left the place on their way back to the castle of Holmwood.

CHAPTER IX.

Believe me,
He is not what he seems, though cause sufficient
Forbids my tongue to utter more of him.—THE CONTRAST.

LEAVING the prisoners and their captors for a time, we must now return to Blanche and her sister, both of whom were waiting in the greatest agony of suspense to hear the result of the expedition which they knew had gone forth in search of the mysterious personage whose presence in the neighbourhood had created so much

apprehension and alarm. The confinement of our heroine was not so close as might have been expected from the anger of her father, and instead of being locked up in crown chamber, she was allowed the full range of the house, on condition that

No. 9.

she did not attempt to leave it till permission had been first obtained from Sir Richard Langdale. Her sister, too, was permitted to be with her, which was an indulgence no less gratifying than it was consolatory under the present gloomy aspect of affairs. Catherine, in short, did all she could to chase away the melancholy thoughts which the mind of her sister, but finding that she still dwelt upon the one subject nearest to her heart, she ventured to question her relative to the stranger upon whom she had placed her affections and confidence.

" Come, dearest Blanche," she exclaimed, " I prithee banish these melancholy reflections of yours, and learn to hope that a better fate awaits your mysterious lover than the fearful one you are so determined to anticipate."

" Alas !" she replied, " though your advice is kindly intended, it is in vain that you urge me to assume an appearance of gaiety that is foreign to my heart. Hunted by his merciless enemies, and surrounded by them on every hand, I can see only the realization of my worst fears."

" Aye," answered Catherine, " but the noble hare, though hardly pressed by his foes, will yet turn when all other resources have failed him, and singly withstand the desperate attacks of those who would hunt him to death."

" The stranger has indeed courage enough," exclaimed Blanche Langdale, " yet what will avail his determined resolution in a case like this? Enraged by the many defeats they have already sustained, his enemies have become more and more inveterate against him; they have resolved upon his destruction, and, incensed by his successful defence, they have devised an hundred cruelties by which to satisfy their thirst for vengeance."

" But do you think he has no chance of escaping the evils you have imagined ?"

" I fear not," answered Blanche ; " the picture is not overdrawn, and such a fate as I have spoken of will, I anticipate, be the fate of him for whom I live."

Catherine paused for a few moments, and then in a voice of gentle persuasion she said :—

" You have often told me, Blanche, that you would ere long confide to me the secret of his name and birth. That neither of them will confer disgrace upon our family I am well convinced ; though the mystery that has ever surrounded him may, to some persons, give rise to a far more unfavourable opinion."

" My dear sister, you shall know all in time," answered Blanche Langdale, " but at present the secret must not—cannot de divulged. That he comes of an honourable family, however, I solemnly pledge my word."

" I believe your assertion," exclaimed Catherine, " but much should I rejoice were it in your power to give the explanation that has been so often asked. Our father—misled by present appearances, and the false representations of interested persons—still persists in denying him a boon which, did he better know him, he might perhaps grant him with pleasure."

" I cannot but acknowledge the truth of what you have said," replied her sister, " yet there are circumstances at present in existence which require him to maintain his incognito."

" But why does he still linger in this neighbourhood, when he so well knows the danger he is in from the malice of those who are arrayed against him as enemies ?"

" His motives I am unable to explain," replied Blanche, " but I know for certain that he is well aware of the conspiracy in which our father is unhappily involved with those bad men who have lately arrived here."

" Was the Outlaw aware of it before he came to seek concealment in the forest of Sherwood ?"

" He knows most of the circumstances connected with it," replied Blanche Langdale, " and sought this neighbourhood to watch over and preserve him from impending ruin."

" Why, then, has he not declared who he is, and why he lurks about so mysteriously ?"

" I have not been favoured with all the secret," answered Blanche ; " but I know enough to assert that, unless he succeeds in rescuing our father from the snare that has been laid for his destruction, he will not disclose himself to the world, even were it to save his own life."

"But, in the meantime," exclaimed Catherine, "this ill-advised plot against the queen and government may chance to be discovered; and in that case our father's ruin and dishonour would be certain to follow."

"The affair," replied her sister, "is already known to those who are most threatened with danger."

"Known!" said Catherine, with alarm. "Are you certain that the motions of the conspirators are watched?"

"There can be no doubt of it."

"And yet," replied the other, "I would fain believe that, in this instance, you have been misinformed."

"Deceive yourself no longer," exclaimed Blanche, "for it is quite impossible that a conspiracy so dangerous as this is, would long escape the vigilant eye of the queen and her ministers."

"Ah! does her majesty know of the disloyalty into which some of her subjects have been betrayed?"

"She does, Catherine," replied her sister; "and, in fact, long since received intelligence of all that is going on amongst those who are conspiring to deprive her of her crown. Nay, even at this very time large bodies of troops are expected to arrive in this neighbourhood for the suppression of a conspiracy that threatens the overthrow of the government.'"

"How know you that troops are expected?" asked Catherine, with visible emotion.

"I was told so by him whom people call the Outlaw."

"Ah!" cried Catherine, "then our father will meet the punishment of a traitor."

"Nay, things will not be so bad as that," answered her sister; "for the supposed Outlaw has, by means of some friend who has influence at court, already succeeded in obtaining for him the promised pardon of the queen. The former long-tried loyalty of Sir Richard Langdale; the services he has performed for his country; and the certainty that he has been blindly led away by men more wicked and designing than himself, have procured for him the wonderful consideration of her majesty; and he, for whose sake your fears have been excited, will be suffered to escape without even the slightest punishment."

"So, at least, you believe, my dear sister," answered Catherine; "but I, who am less sanguine, fear the consequences will be more serious than you imagine."

"Such," replied her sister, "is the information I have received from our mysterious visitor; and I do not believe that he would have asserted it except upon the most certain grounds."

At this juncture shouts, like those of triumph, rent the air; and before the two females could reach the window to see what was the matter, Nicodemus Dove, breathless and overjoyed, came running towards them.

"Oh, young ladies," he exclaimed, clapping his hands with delight, "I bring you such capital news—we've done it—we've done it! and the rascal will swing for his crimes as sure as he's got a head on his shoulders."

"In the name of goodness! what have you done?" demanded the half-terrified Blanche Langdale. "You speak of having performed some important feat, yet leave us to guess what has taken place. For goodness sake, Mr. Dove, explain yourself that we may no longer be kept in this state of suspense—you spoke of having done something, now tell us what you have done?"

"What have we done?" echoed the other. "Why we have done the Outlaw to be sure."

"Again I must request you to explain yourself," cried Blanche, with increasing alarm.

"Well, then, we've made the Outlaw our prisoner."

"A prisoner!"

"Yes; he's safe enough now, I can tell you," answered Nicodemus Dove; "he won't get his liberty again very easily, I can tell you, nor——but I say, Miss Blanche, you don't seem to be at all pleased with the news I have brought."

"Pleased !"

"Yes," he replied, "for my own part I'm quite delighted—quite inspired by the affair. Ah! young ladies, you shall see in a few days what a beautiful poem I'll write upon the subject."

"This heartless levity, Mr. Dove," exclaimed Catherine, with marked emphasis, might, and would have been spared, had you entertained the slightest regard for me or my sister."

"Regard !" echoed the poet—"why don't I love you both?—and haven't I proved it by writing sonnets and odes on your hair and eyes, in spite of all you can say against it?—Regard, forsooth!—have you no recollection of that last poem of mine, beginning with these lines :—

> "Dear girls I love you both—
> But can't make up my mind
> Which maid shall have my troth
> Because young love is blind.
> I fain would wed the pair—"

"Mr. Dove," exclaimed Blanche, interrupting his effusion, "your insults, or your folly, I know not which it may be, is no longer to be endured with patience. Leave us, sir, or my father shall resent your intolerable impertinence."

"Well, but my dear young lady," persisted Nicodemus," you'll allow me to stay I suppose till I have told you all. Your father, as lord of the forest district, is going to try the Outlaw for his misdemeanours."

"Has he the power to do so?" asked Blanche.

"To be sure he has," answered Nicodemus Dove. "They are already assembling in the great hall for the purpose of proceeding with the trial immediately— and woe be to the prisoner if they find him guilty !"

"Surely," cried Blanche, with alarm, "my father will not venture to send a fellow creature to death without giving him the fair trial to which all persons are entitled."

"I don't much think that anything you can say will save him from death ; his enemies have a chance of sending him to the gibbet without getting themselves into trouble."

"At all events," sighed Blanche Langdale, "no effort shall be spared to release him from this difficulty. My father knows the consequences of exciting the queen's anger, and he will pause ere he commits an act that would bring ruin upon him."

"It's all very well for you to think so, young lady," exclaimed Nicodemus; "but you may take my word for it that they'll hang him up on the highest tree in your father's park, in less than an hour from the time of his conviction.

> "When once they find him guilty—
> He'll have no other hope,
> They'll take him to the greenwood tree
> And hang him with a rope."

Disgusted with his conduct, the two sisters made their way towards the door, but ere they took their departure, Blanche cast a withering glance of scorn at him, as she exclaimed :—

"Your insolence and brutality, sir, are no longer to be endured by those whose feelings you would trifle. You seek to wound the hearts of two unprotected females, and by your unfounded prognostications of the future endeavour to plunge them into sorrow, deeper even than that which already afflicts them. My father shall, however, hear of your conduct, in order that he may resent it in the manner it best deserves."

"Nay, fair Blanche," he cried, "don't fly into such a confounded passion, but hear what I have to say, and—"

"I will hear nothing," she replied, "for you have proved yourself unworthy of the friendship with which you were received beneath this roof. Be assured, Sir Richard Langdale shall hear of it, and if he has not lost all regard for his daughters he will without delay command you to quit his house."

And so saying, she took the arm of her sister Catherine, and left the poet not a little amazed at the unexpected turn that affairs had taken against him."

"Hoity, toity!" he at length exclaimed, "did anybody ever hear such a young vixen as that. It's all very pretty and sentimental I dare say, and would be a capital subject for an epic poem, in twenty-four cantos; but its plain enough that Miss Blanche is a bit of a shrew in her way, and my prospects of wedded happiness are not quite so bright and promising as they were. I must reflect before the step is taken; and as for Sir Richard, I must see him, and soften down his anger if the girl tries, as she threatened to do—to make mischief between us. But hark! there's more bustle going on in the hall, so I must be off or the trial will be over, and I not present to witness what goes on."

Upon this, he was running out of the room, when Arnheim and Father Francis suddenly presented themselves before him.

"Nicodemns Dove," exclaimed the priest, "we have come hither in search of the ladies, who, we were informed, were in this apartment."

"It is their father's will, that they attend the trial of the Outlaw in the great hall."

"Why they have only just now left me," answered the person who had been addressed, "and it's most likely they've gone there, for Miss Blanche said something about going to seek her father."

"Indeed," said the priest with surprise, "do you know for what purpose they want to seek him?"

"I can pretty well guess," answered the other, "but I would rather not say anything about it, till I know whether my surmise is correct. However, its very certain, that Blanche Langdale is in a marvellous deal of trouble about the capture of her sweetheart, and if he should be condemned to die, I've a notion, that she would not survive him very long."

"And die he will," exclaimed Arnheim, "for our friend Henry Neville hates him as a rival, and Sir Richard owes him a grudge for daring to pay his addresses to his daughter."

"And there is small chance of his escaping," added the priest.

"Were you present when he was taken?" inquired Nicodemus Dove, of the last speaker.

"I was not," he replied, "and most heartily do I congratulate myself upon the chance that led me in another direction."

"Humph! You are prepossessed in favour of the mysterious stranger then it seems?"

"I confess it," exclaimed Father Francis, "for there is something in the noble bearing of the person you speak of, that proclaims him to be better than he seems."

"Ah!" observed Nicodemus, with marked emphasis, "that's the case with a great many other persons that I could mention, for they talk of a conspiracy against the queen, and I have my own suspicions, that some of her enemies are lurking about in the neighbourhood of this place."

"Are there any persons that you suspect in particular?" asked the priest, unable to disguise his alarm.

"Yes—to tell you the truth, there are several."

"May I inquire who they are."

"You may ask what questions you please," returned Nicodemus, "but I shall not mention the names of any of the persons, though, between ourselves, Father Francis, I have one or two of them in my eye, at this very moment."

"What mean you?" exclaimed the priest, startled by these words, "whom you suspec?"

" I've said, that I shall not mention any names just yet," replied Nicodemus Dove, " but I know there are spies and villains, who are going about the country, deluding the queen's subjects with lies, and urging them on to treason."

" Are you sure that your suspicions are correct?" demanded Arnheim, no less alarmed than his companion.

" I'm pretty certain about it," replied the poet, " and as I happen to be a loyal subject of her majesty's, I intend to watch the rascals closely. They fancy that everything is going on snugly, but by-and-by, when they least suspect it, they'll find themselves as firmly in the arms of the law, that nothing will save them from the gibbet."

" The gibbet," groaned Arnheim,—and then recovering an appearance of composure, he added—" Perhaps, my good friend, your suspicions about this conspiracy are founded in moonshine, and then there will be no occasion for the gibbet. Besides, it may be, that the arms of the law that you speak of, will be neither long or strong enough to hold them."

" Aye," replied Nicodemus knowingly, " that may happen to be the case with the laws over in your country, Mr. German; but let me tell you, that we, in England, manage such matters a great deal better. Here the laws are held in respect, for even the sovereign is not allowed to slight it altogether."

" How is it then," asked the priest, " that some of your people set the laws at open defiance?"

" I don't understand you."

" How does it happen," continued the priest, " that our great men so frequently perform deeds of cruelty and oppression, that would not be tolerated if impartial justice was the rule observed by your country people?"

" Will you have the kindness to explain what you mean?" cried Nicodemus Dove.

" That can be easily done," answered the other. " Why, for instance, we need look no further off than our worthy poet, Sir Richard Langdale. He assumes to himself the power of a sovereign, and would even now provide a feast for the ravens, by hanging the Outlaw upon his own responsibility.'

" True—you are right enough there, i'faith," exclaimed Nicodemus; " yet still I mean to contend that for that act, Sir Richard will deserve the gratitude of his country."

" On what ground?"

" That the man deserves hanging, to be sure."

" Are you sure of it?"

" Why, of course, I am," exclaimed Nicodemus Dove; " our host may hang up the Outlaw, and if he does so, the deed will be a meritorious one, and deserves the approbation of her majesty."

" Do you speak advisedly?"

" To be sure I do."

" Perhaps then, sir, you will have the goodness to tell me why the man should be hanged?"

" Well, then," replied Nicodemus, " it somehow strikes me—and I'm not very often mistaken in my judgment—that this Outlaw is nothing more nor less than one of the conspirators I was just now talking about."

" Indeed!" exclaimed the priest, somewhat reassured by what he had heard; " there is some probability in this suggestion of yours, but have you anything to offer in the way of proof?"

" Not much at present," answered the other; " but the fellow has been seen sneaking about the neighbourhood for some time past; and, as I said before, it's well known that some of the traitors are lurking in these parts. However, luckily enough, the chap is now in safe custody, and all I hope is that they won't fail to fit him speedily with a hempen cravat."

" You are right, my boy!" exclaimed Arnheim, grasping him by the hand. " I dare say he is one of the villains that have been plotting against the queen's life, and her majesty is fortunate in having subjects of such sagacity as you possess to protect her interest and check the evil designs of her enemies."

"Ay, ay," replied Nicodemus, flattered by the compliment that had been paid him; "I believe there are very few that can boast of more acuteness than myself."

"But are you convinced?" asked the priest, "have you any proofs by which the crime of treason may be brought home to the person of whom we are speaking?"

"Leave the proofs to my management," answered Nicodemus, "and you will see how nicely the whole plot will be brought out. I kuow the work I have got to do and her majesty shall not have cause to say that Nicodemus Dove has done it carelessly. I know the fellow to be a traitor, and I'll never leave him till he has met his deserts on the gallows."

"Yet I can see no sufficient reason for suspecting that he is concerned in a plot against the state."

"But I do, though," answered the poet; "if he was not a rogue—an emissary—a traitor to his queen and country—if he were really an honest man, why does he not come openly and pay his addresses to Blanche Langdale?"

"There may be a reason for it," exclaimed the priest, "very different from those you have mentioned."

"Ah! you are deceived in him, depend upon it. Besides, hasn't he been hiding himself at the cottage of that wild woodman, Stephen Dagley, who, with his wife, son, and daughter, are all taken up and are to be tried together?"

"No, no, there you are wrong," interposed Arnheim.

"Wrong! why they were brought prisoners to the castle."

"True, but Sir Richard Langdale has thought proper, for some reason or another, to pardon all but the Outlaw, and he, I am thinking will have but a poor chance of saving his life."

"And the Dagleys," continued Father Francis, "refuse to leave the castle till they know the fate of the mysterious personage they have sheltered and protected."

"Then if I was Sir Richard Langdale," observed the poet, "I'd have them all turned out neck and crop."

"On the contrary," answered Father Francis, "our worthy host has yielded to their solicitations, and they are permitted to remain as spectators of the trial."

"Then Sir Richard is a greater fool than I took him for," exclaimed Nicodemus Dove, "for depend upon it there'll be a desperate attempt to rescue the prisoner, and if once he escapes it's not very likely that he will be caught again very soon. Besides, they're all of 'em together a bad lot, and the best thing that could have been done would be to make an example of 'em."

"Upon my word, friend," observed the priest, "you seem to hold very vindictive feelings against those people."

"I'm not at all vindictive," answered the poet, "but all the interest of the plot will be lost if some of them are not hanged."

"Interest!" exclaimed Father Francis with surprise.

"Yes," replied the other, "the truth is, I had a thought of turning the subject into verse, but if Sir Richard don't hang a few of the people, the poem won't be worth writing. A desperate tragedy where all your principal characters are killed off, is your only true test of a man of genius like myself."

"Well, well, my friend," said the priest, "yonr favours of invention must take flight in some other direction. For the present you must forget your poetry, and accompany us to the chamber, where the trial of the Outlaw is to take place."

"I'm quite ready to go with you, gentlemen," answered Nicodemus, "but as to forgetting my poetry, that's quite impossible. Only think of my opening lines— after a *line* of another description has done the Outlaw's business.

"Near Holinwood hall there roved a blade,
     A very daring chap;
And stealing deers, sirs, was his trade,
     Till they laid for him a trap;
  They captured him, and—"

But never mind the rest at present, gentlemen, the remainder of my ry must be told when I know whether they mean to hang the prisoner or not.'

Arnheim and the priest had, however, left the room during the recital of his verses, and following them with no little chagrin at the want of taste they had displayed, he was accosted by Dame Dagley, who, like himself, was proceeding towards the Hall, where the trial was to take place. Nicodemus would have avoided her, but she knew his intention, and held him firmly by the arm.

"I must speak to you," she exclaimed, "for you are a friend of Sir Richard Langdale, and may have influence enough over him to prevent the commission of a deed that he will have reason bitterly to repent. Tell me, is he serious in the intention of putting the stranger to death?"

"If by the stranger you mean the Outlaw," answered Nicodemus, "I can assure you that Sir Richard is determined, upon proof of guilt, to send him to the gallows."

"Let him beware then," exclaimed Dame Dagley, "for if he proceeds to that extent he will create enemies amongst those who will never rest till they have satisfied their revenge."

"My good woman, I have nothing to do with that," replied the other, "Sir Richard Langdale is his own master, and he knows his own business better than any body can tell him; and as for interfering between him and his will, I'd as soon think of walking into a den of wild beasts."

"But you can remonstrate with him against committing a crime like this."

"Nay, I don't see any great crime in hanging a deer-stealer," exclaimed Nicodemus Dove; "the fellow has had his way long enough, I think, and, now that they've got him fast, I hope they'll carry the law to its very utmost extent."

"And if they do," answered the woman, "it will be the worst day's work Sir Richard ever did for himself."

"Psha! he don't mind the ravings of a mad woman."

"He may not heed my words," exclaimed Dame Dagley, "but he will be sorry for it when repentance comes too late."

"Why do you take up this matter so warmly?" asked Nicodemus.

"Because I hate tyranny, let it be practised by whom it may."

"Humph! by your language I suppose you are concerned in the plot against the queen?"

"The queen has not a more loyal subject in her dominions than myself," replied Dame Dagley; "I love and would protect her, and woe to those who are conspiring against her majesty, for I know some of the traitors, and will hurl confusion upon them when least a discovery is expected!"

"If you know anything about it," exclaimed Nicodemus, "perhaps you will have no objection to let me into the secret?"

"None will know of it till the proper moment arrives," answered the woman. "On that subject however, I have nothing more to say at present. My object just now is to save the life of the Outlaw, and as that can only be done through Sir Richard Langdale, I would entreat your interest with him, in order that a cold-blooded murder may be prevented."

"Upon my life, Mistress Dagley, I have no interest with him."

"Are you not about to become the husband of one of his daughters?"

"I thought so at one time, I must confess," answered Nicodemus Dove, "but matters begin to look very queer, unless the young lady should relent after her other lover—the Outlaw—has been sent to the gallows."

"And have you the presumption," she asked scornfully, "to be the rival of the stranger?"

"Presumption!—do you imagine that I place myself upon a level with the Outlaw?"

"That I know you cannot do," she replied, "for he is far above you, though, for reasons of his own he cannot just now reveal himself to the world."

"It's all very easy for him to say so," replied Nicodemus, "but we only know him as an outlaw and a deer-stealer, and if his guilt is proved to the satisfaction of Sir Richard Langdale, his life won't be worth any very long purchase."

"As a friend of Sir Richard's, it is your duty to warn him that his own death will shortly follow that of his prisoner."

"Upon my word, Mrs. Dagley," exclaimed the poet, "if you go on talking in that way, I shall begin to think that you have some design against him yourself."

"Think as you please," she replied, "but do not on any account neglect the hint I have told you to give him. It is not the part of a woman to pursue revenge to the extent I have spoken of; but there are other persons who will take the life of Sir Richard Langdale, if he persists in sending his prisoner to the gibbet."

"Perhaps your husband or son have threatened to do my friend a mischief?"

"If it were so," she replied, "it is hardly likely that I should reveal the secret, since Sir Richard already owes them a grudge that he would like to have the opportunity of putting into execution. There are, however, more people than my

No. 10.

husband or son who would revenge the death of the outlaw within a few hours after the tragedy was over."

" Then why haven't you told Sir Richard so ?"

" Because he is too proud and too great for a poor person like myself to approach."

" But surely neither his pride nor his greatness would be allowed to interfere in a matter of life and death ?"

" I don't know how that might be," returned the dame, " but if you have any regard for his safety you will not fail to put him upon his guard against the danger that threatens him. At all events, you profess to love his daughter, and for her sake you must endeavour to preserve her only protector."

" How can I do that," asked Nicodemus Dove, " if there are three persons looking out to do him an injury ?"

" Easily," she replied ; " tell him to give liberty to the outlaw, and I can answer for it he will have nothing to fear from those who are now sworn to hurl destruction on him."

" Do you think he would believe me if I was to throw out such a hint as you have suggested ?"

" There need be no reserve, as far as I am concerned," replied Dame Dagley ; " and, therefore, he will have no reason to doubt that the warning is not given from any interested motive. Say that you received your information from me, and he will no longer hesitate as to which course he ought to pursue."

" I don't know that," answered the poet ; " for he happens to be rather obstinate, and may imagine that you have some motive of your own to serve in this instance."

" My only motive is to save the life of a man whom I know to be innocent."

" How can you know that he is innocent," asked Nicodemus, " when we have abundant proofs every day that he lawlessly kills deer in the neighbouring forest ?"

" To answer that question," she replied, " would require more explanation than I have just now a right to give. Let it suffice that he is here for the purpose of concealment, and I believe nothing will induce him to discover himself till he can clear his name from the foul dishonour that certain of his enemies have heaped upon it."

" Hah !" exclaimed the other ; " but I'm thinking he'll be glad to say who he is when he finds that there is no other way left to save his neck from the halter."

" Believe it not," she replied, " for, from all I have seen and heard, he would rather perish by an ignominious death than bring shame upon the noble name he bears."

" A noble name ! Why, what is he but an outlaw ?"

" It is in vain to ask me," exclaimed the woman, " because, even if I were in the secret, I have resolution enough to remain silent as long as he is in danger. All I require is, that you will exert your influence with Sir Richard Langdale to save the life of his unfortunate prisoner."

" And what good should I get by that ?"

" You would have the consolation of saving the life of an innocent and persecuted man," she replied. " Besides, Catherine Langdale would be grateful to the preserver of her sister's lover, and the chances are that she might be prevailed upon to accept your addresses, which have hitherto been proffered in vain. Think of it, and fail not to exert whatever influence you may possess in behalf of the prisoner."

By this time they had reached the door of the great hall, and, abruptly breaking off the conversation, she quitted her hold of the poet, and glided into the Chamber of Justice.

CHAPTER X.

By what law,
By whose authority am I thus forced
To plead my guilt or innocence ?—DON RAYMOND.

WHEN the two persons we have named entered the hall of trial, most of the principal persons concerned in the examination of the Outlaw were assembled, and had taken their allotted places. Sir Richard Langdale, as judge, was seated on a canopied chair at the head of the table, and in his immediate vicinity stood Henry Neville, Arnheim, and Father Francis, with all of whom he seemed to be busily engaged in conversation. The remainder of the hall was filled with the retainers who had assembled to witness the proceedings. A little in advance of their father sat Blanche Langdale and her sister, and on the other side of the table stood Stephen Dagley, who was now joined by his wife and his son and daughter; Dame Dagley, however, appeared to be the most anxious of the party and being almost unobserved, she murmured to herself,—

" The hour has now arrived. when the Outlaw must either perish as a felon, or his name be revealed to secure his safety from these bitter foes. But there are yet those at hand who will do their best to save him in his utmost need. A few brief moments more will see the queen's troops admitted within the strong walls of Holmwood Castle, and that too, while their gaping menials are witnessing the trial of him who has thus been prosecuted as an Outlaw. But I must recover myself for the last act of this drama, which is to terminate so differently to what was expected by the exulting enemies of the prisoner. And see ! the business for which they have been assembled is about to commence."

She withdrew herself a little from observation, and as she did so, Sir Richard Langdale, addressing himself to the assemblage before him, exclaimed,—

" Friends and neighbours, we are met to pronounce judgment upon the Outlaw, who has so long set us at open defiance. He has destroyed my deer and lorded it over my keepers ; and, as if that were not enough, he has planned the abduction of my daughter, whom I esteem as even dearer than life itself. I know you have all too much regard for me to expect that I shall sit down patiently with this indignity ; and having the award of justice in my own hand I will do myself right, let the consequences of my act be what they may. My prisoner hath braved all ventures, and he must now bide his doom, though I could fain have wished that justice could have been more easily satisfied."

" Are there any persons here," demanded Sir Richard, " who have aught to urge against the acknowledged prerogative which I maintain over those who commit evil upon my estate ?"

No answer was returned to this, and amidst the solemn silence that ensued, the baronet motioned to two or three of his retainers and bade them to bring forth the prisoner."

" Ay," exclaimed Nicodemus Dove, " let him be brought forth by all means, that he may answer for the high crimes and misdemeanours he has been guilty of. He would have married the lady heiress of these broad acres, and—

" Peace, prating idiot !" interrupted Henry Neville ; " peace, I say, or my sword shall ensure your silence."

" I shall not hold my tongue for you," retorted the poet indignantly. " This place belongs to Sir Richard Langdale, and by no other person will I be put down."

Here the altercation was interrupted by the entrance of the Outlaw, guarded by those who had been dispatched to fetch him. For a moment or two he glanced proudly around upon the assemblage, and then, without betraying the slightest emotion or fear, took his place on the spot which was pointed out to him by one of the baronet's principal retainers. Nicodemus Dove appeared to take great interest in all that was going forward, and whispering to the next bystander, he said,—

"He's a tolerably good-looking chap, at any rate, and Miss Blanche, I'll be bound, is not the only woman that has looked kindly on him."

"Perhaps so," answered the other, in a low tone, lest he should be overheard by the baronet; Nicodemus, however, had no such fear, and still thinking upon his one all-engrossing subject, he continued,—

"He looks like a bit of a genius, too, though I don't suppose he ever wrote any poetry to the lady, praising the beauty of her complexion, and the richness of her clustering ringlets; and yet, why should I expect it, when it aint everybody that understands the art of rhyming LOVES and DOVES, and all that sort of thing."

"Has care been taken to disarm this man?"

"He has been carefully searched and all weapons have been taken away from him," answered the person addressed.

"Your task has been ill performed then," continued Neville, "for methinks I can discover something in the form of a dagger concealed beneath his cloak."

"Let him be searched," exclaimed Sir Richard Langdale; "not that we have any reason to fear him; but, felon as he is, he has no right to be in the possession of arms.

A momentary working of the countenance showed these remarks had stung the Outlaw to the quick, and glancing fiercely towards the last speaker, he said with impassioned emphasis,

"Who is't that dares brand me with the name of felon?" Sir Richard Langdale, you are a much older man than myself, else by the worth of my honour this insult would have cost the life of either you or myself."

"Humph," ejaculated Henry Neville, "that word *honour* has been foully disgraced, coming, as it does, from one who stands but a short distance from the gibbet.

Honour, indeed! what do you rate it at? a thief's honour is a novelty that I never heard of before. Nay, Sir Outlaw, bite your lips as much as you please,— I say thief, robber, cut-purse, for you are all of those and each in particular."

The Outlaw made two or three violent efforts to break from those who held him in custody; and Sir Richard Langdale, fearing the consequences that might ensue, endeavoured to mediate between them.

"Peace, both of you, I command," he exclaimed, rising abruptly from his seat, "for I will maintain the dignity of my office even that it be enforced by sending my friend to one of the castle dungeons. And you," he continued, addressing himself to the Outlaw, "what have you to say in your defence against the charge that is now brought against you?" What excuse can you offer for having abused my honour, and stained the hitherto unsullied dignity of my house?"

"I am not guilty of either of the charges you have thought proper to bring against me," answered the prisoner, as he drew himself up into a firm and dignified posture.

"Have you not endeavoured to gain the affections of a girl far your superior in life?"

"That I have loved—that I do love your daughter," answered the Outlaw, "I would not deny though the confession itself brought me instant death. But both her honour and yours, for me, are as pure as heaven."

"For *you*, sirrah," exclaimed the enraged baronet, "and who, pray, are you?"

"That is an explanation which, under present circumstances, I do not think proper to give."

"Nay, but thou shalt," said Sir Richard Langdale; "for if thou wouldst save thy life, thou must declare thy name and where thou comest. What," he added tauntingly, as the prisoner remained perfectly silent; "hast thou no lie ready by which to carry on thy vile deception?"

"A lie, Sir Richard!"

"Ay, that was the word I said."

"Well, well," exclaimed the Outlaw, recovering his calmness, though not without an effort, "I can bear for awhile with your taunts and insults. What I am, and who I am, I will not tell to any person here."

"In that case," cried Sir Richard Langdale, "I shall hesitate no longer to exert an authority with which I am armed. It is my privilege to try those persons who are found guilty of commiting offences on my estate, and in virtue of that I adjudge you to the death of a felon. Seize him, guards, and bear him without delay to the court-yard, whilst some of you erect a gibbet for the execution of my sentence."

The men approached to obey this command, but the Outlaw instantly started back, and throwing himself into an attitude of resistance, exclaimed,—

"Stand off all of you! stand back, I say, for I can be resolute in my own cause, and will not tamely yield whilst life remains within me! If I must die, I will at least have the satisfaction of slaying some of those who attempted to lay hands upon me. You see, Sir Richard," he continued exultingly, "your people advance not, and would rather obey my commands than yours."

"Cowards!" said the enraged baronet, "why do you stand as if appalled by his presence? Seize him, I say; and, as your own lives will answer for it, let not the execution of his sentence be delayed another instant."

Urged by these threats the men seemed to be evidently preparing themselves for a simultaneous attack upon him, the Outlaw, however, was resolved to defend himself to the last, and snatching the sword which hung by the side of Nicodemus Dove, he instantly assumed a defensive attitude.

"By Heavens!" he exclaimed, "I will not tamely submit whilst I have strength to wield this weapon in my own defence."

"Submit," roared Henry Neville, almost maddened by the fear manifested amongst the retainers.

"Submit I never will," answered the Outlaw, "and he who first ventures to approach me dies at my feet! Now, fellows, let any one among you advance upon me and I will cleave him from skull to brisket!"

"Nay, then," exclaimed Henry Neville, "if there's no other way to master you, take this to your heart."

As he gave utterance to these words he drew a pistol from his belt, and forcing a passage through the crowd, levelled his weapon at the breast of the Outlaw. At that moment of imminent peril, however, Dame Dagley rushed frantically forward, and seizing the pistol suddenly, succeeded in wresting it from his grasp, then throwing herself between Henry Neville and the Outlaw, who presented the weapon at the former, at the same time exclaiming —

"Now, Henry Neville,—approach but another hair's breadth from the spot on which you stand, and your own life shall pay the forfeit of your temerity."

"By Heavens, I will not be disappointed of my revenge!" cried the young man fiercely. "Arnheim, and all who profess yourselves to be my friends, delay not another moment, but aid me in my cause. Take him alive if possible, but at any rate let him not triumph over us."

Spurred on by these words, Arnheim, at the head of several of the retainers dashed desperately forward, as Stephen Dagley and his son placed themselves by the side of the Outlaw with the intention of sacrificing themselves in his behalf. At that critical juncture, however, the sound of a bugle was heard without in the court yard, and all stood transfixed with wonder and alarm. In another moment a party of the queen's soldiers came into the hall, and the officer in command, advancing quickly between the contending parties, made a sign for both sides to lower their arms.

"Hold!—madmen that you are," he exclaimed; "why are your swords drawn against this man?"

"We know him to be a robber and a spoiler," answered Sir Richard Langdale, "and therefore have I used my privilege to condemn him to the death he merits. He has, however, resisted my people, and it was under my orders that my people were about to slay him to prevent the mischief that would have followed his escape."

"He is neither a robber nor a spoiler," exclaimed the officer, "and therefore your words have done him a foul injustice."

"Who is he then?" demanded Sir Richard.

"One," replied the officer, "who owns a fairer name and higher honour than any of those who thus seek to brand his name with ignominy and crime."

"You hear what is said," exclaimed Sir Richard, addressing himself to the Outlaw. "This gentleman vouches for your unsullied honour, and it now only remains for you to prove the truth of his assertions by declaring your name and family in the presence of this assemblage."

"Since there is no further motive for maintaining my disguise, I will at once freely disclose myself," answered the Outlaw, and then throwing aside his cloak, he appeared habited in the rich garb which betokened him to be of high lineage. In me," he added to the wondering spectators, "you behold the Earl of Danvers!"

"The Earl of Danvers!" murmured the crowd with surprise.

"Ay," he replied, "it is even so, and but for the fortunate arrival of these soldiers I should have been sacrificed to the evil passions of those who sought my life. For the violence and enmity of my rival Henry Neville, I can find some excuse, but I am at a loss to account for the revengeful animosity of Sir Richard Langdale, whom I have never injured."

"My Lord Danvers," exclaimed the baronet, who by this time had somewhat recovered from his surprise, "I had little expected to see a nobleman of your exalted rank masquerading under the assumed characters of a midnight robber, and an outlaw."

"Nor would you, Sir Richard," answered the other, "had it not been for the feud that has existed between your family and mine."

"And you thought by this scheme to heal the difference that existed between us?"

"The situation in which I found myself placed," replied the earl, "may excuse the step into which I was driven. For some months past I have loved your daughter, Blanche, but the enmity that has hitherto held our houses apart, forbade all hope of making her my bride. That thought was madness to me; and, as my only alternative, I adopted this ruse in the hope of obtaining occcasional interviews with her from whom I could not endure the thoughts of a separation."

"Then there's an end of the romance of the thing at once," whispered Nicodemus Dove, to the person who stood nearest to him. "If he's no outlaw there can be no hanging, and the poem, I had commenced upon the subject, has received its death-blow."

"And a very good thing too," muttered Stephen Dagley, who happened to hav overheard, "for your friends will be spared an infliction that would have been worse than a three days' ague."

During this brief interval, Sir Richard Langdale appeared to be struggling with his feelings, but at length yielding to his better nature, he advanced towards the recently discovered nobleman, and grasping him by the hand, exclaimed,—

"Well, well, my lord, pardon that which is past, and for the future I hope we shall be friends. I regret all that has occurred, but henceforth you shall have nothing to reproach me with."

"I joyfully accept your proffered friendship," answered Lord Danvers, "and my happiness would be complete could I but be assured that no further obstacles exist to my union with your daughter Blanche."

"In all probability you have nothing to fear from any opposition on my part," answered Sir Richard Langdale;—"nay, I will at once remove all doubt upon the subject by giving my consent to your union. You love my daughter, and as I know the passion is reciprocal, there is no reason to believe that she will refuse to obey the command of her father." Thus beckoning for Blanche to approach, he joined their hands and continued, with some emotion:—"I trust, my lord, your union will heal the feuds that have hitherto existed between us. Henceforth, I trust, all animosity will cease to exist."

"For myself I can answer," replied his lordship, "and never can I forget the heavy debt of gratitude that your kindness has laid me under. From this moment let us both forget the bitter feelings with which we have been used to regard each other."

" Be it so," exclaimed Sir Richard Langdale ;—" but there is one question that I have yet to ask:—What means this intrusion of an armed body of men within the walls of Holmwood Castle?"

"Perhaps I am best able to answer that question," interposed the o ... in command. " We visit Holmwood, Sir Richard Langdale, not for the apprehension of known traitors, but for the prevention of a dangerous plot against the state."

" What mean you, sir?" demanded the baronet, turning pale with terror at these words.

" I mean," answered the other, " that the conspiracy in which you have been engaged, has reached the ears of the queen."

" And your orders are to arrest me as a traitor ?"

" No," replied the officer, " her majesty having dispatched me hither with as armed band, commands me to say thus :—Sir Richard Langdale and his associaten are pardoned even before they sue for mercy."

" Pardoned !" exclaimed the baronet ; " does her majesty then pardon us all?"

" Hear me out, I pray," resumed the officer. " *You*, she freely and uncondi- tionally forgives ; but Henry Neville, Colonel Arnheim, and Father Francis must quit the shores of England for ever."

" And why," demanded Henry Neville, " is this difference made between us when we are all equally guilty ?".

" I am not in her majesty's confidence," replied the officer, " and therefore am not able to answer your question. All that I know is, that you and your com- panions must embark for a foreign country within fourteen days, and in the mea time you have permission to visit the mansion of your father, who, it is not likely you will ever see again. Your friends will also be suffered to remain at liberty, but in order to prevent a repetition of their treachery, a strict watch will be kept over their actions till they take their departure from this country. You see, there- fore, that the queen is not revengeful, even against her enemies."

" Do you know," asked Sir Richard, " to what circumstance we owe this royal clemency ?"

" I do not," answered the other ; " but I suppose she is so well assured of the loyalty and attachment of the great majority of her subjects, that she can afford to be magnanimous, when she sees how few have engaged in this conspiracy. And now, Sir Richard Langdale, having performed the errand on which I was sent, I will take my leave with a solemn warning to yourself and your colleagues, to shew your gratitude for her majesty's gracious pardon, by no more attempts to disturb the peace of the realm she governs."

" You will be pleased to convey my grateful thanks to the queen for her royal mercy," said the baronet ; " and tell her, that from henceforth, whenever there may be occasion for it, my sword shall be drawn in her defence."

" She is assured of it, Sir Richard," exclaimed the other, " or the offence you have been guilty of, would not have been so easily pardoned. Had there been a doubt upon the subject, you, and your fellow traitors would have been, by thi time on the road to the Tower of London. However, I congratulate you upon your escape, and I trust, these other gentlemen will not disobey the royal command, that orders them to quit England within the space of fourteen days."

" For my own part," muttered Henry Neville, " I feel no regret at leaving a coun- try in which I can no longer live in honour. Towards the queen personally, I entertain no feeling of disloyalty; but the religion is not that of my father's, and it was to restore the old mode of worship that I joined with a few others in this plot."

. " Ay," exclaimed Arnheim, " and it would have been successful too, but for some traitor in our camp who h s betrayed our design to the queen. However, as the affair has been discovered, I shall obey the command to quit the realm, and as there are wars going on abroad, I shall soon find employment congenial to my mind."

" And to prove that I am not ungrateful for the mercy of your sovereign," added Father Francis, " I would have you warn her, that there are many others in this nny, besides ourselves, who are anxiously looking out for the time, when the religion of Rome will be predominant in this country. I give you this hint for he own benefit, that she may be npon her guard ngainst future conspiracies."

" Her majesty is well enough aware of all that," answered the officer, " but she has wise councillors and loyal subjects, upon whom she can depend in cas o emergency. Had she been less prepared, the plot, in which you were concernedf might not have been discovered till too late."

" I hope her majesty don't suspect that I have had any hand in it," exclaimed Nicodemus Dove, for the first time venturing to thrust himself forward."

" You may depend upon it she does not," answered the officer, smiling; " for though she had been informed that a certain Nicodemus Dove was one of the visitors at Holmwood castle, she needed little inquiry to convince her that no danger was to be apprehended from him."

" Perhaps," continued the poet, " you will have the kindness to tell her that I knew nothing of what was going on in the castle, though it must be confessed I had my suspicions that there was mischief in the wind somewhere. In short, Mr. Officer, they knew my loyalty too well to let me have a notion that a plot was going on against her most gracious majesty."

" He is right enough there," exclaimed Henry Neville, " for knowing him to be a busy, meddling fool, we were most careful to keep the secret from his knowledge."

" So, I'm a busy, meddling fool am I ?" cried the indignant bard. " You call me hard names, Master Neville, " but, wise as you may be yourself, I can challenge you any day to sit down and write such poetry as I do."

" A truce to this foolish wrangling," interposed Sir Richard Langdale; " for we have at present more important matters for our consideration. Have we not just escaped from danger, and shall we now ferment quarrels, that after all can only end in ridicule ?"

" There's no fear of my exchanging many angry words with an insignificant fellow like that," exclaimed Henry Neville. " If a quarrel takes place, it should be between you and me, for I have reason enough for dissatisfaction, seeing that you have so suddenly changed your mind with respect to who shall be the husband of your daughter."

" And have I not a right to change my mind under such circumstances as these ?" demanded the baronet. " Shall I give her to a man who is to be an exile for life, or bestow her upon one who is high in favour with his sovereign, and of whose attendance I have had such proofs ?"

" Yet half an hour since," answered the other bitterly, " and you would have sent him to the gibbet as a felon."

" Right," exclaimed Sir Richard; " but since the discovery of his name and rank, I see reason enough to rejoice that the injustice I was about to commit has been prevented. You, Henry Neville, have been disappointed of obtaining the hand of a wealthy heiress, but since I believe you bore her no great love, you will now have an opportunity of looking out for some other female whom you can regard with that affection which alone can render the marriage state happy."

Neville would not trust himself to make any reply to this, and beckoning to his two companions, he left the room muttering his curses against the baronet. Immediately afterwards the officer and his guard also retired, when the Earl of Danvers, taking the hand of the baronet, exclaimed—

" Sir Richard, I heartily congratulate you on your providential escape from the hands of those designing men. The queen has granted her pardon, though she cannot acquit you of all blame ; and your future life will, I doubt not, justify the high opinion she has been pleased to honour you with."

" Her majesty shall see that I am not ungrateful for the clemency with which she has viewed my offence," answered the other ; " and from this time forth I will studiously avoid the society of those who bear her ill will. In short, my lord, I never entered with much zeal into this plot, and had any other thing than the restoration of the old religion been the object, I should have refused to give it my countenance and support."

" I can see," exclaimed the Earl of Danvers, " that Henry Neville has been the chief mover in this sedition, and he has therefore little cause to complain of the sentence which expels him from his country. But for the intercession of his father who is in high favour at court, he would in all probability have paid the forfeit of his crime on the scaffold."

"But her Majesty has been equally lenient with the two foreigners," observed Sir Richard.

"She was in some degree compelled to be so," answered the nobleman; "for having inflicted a comparatively light punishment upon the chief person engaged in the plot, it would have appeared unjust had she proceeded with more rigour against those who were in the employ of Henry Neville. Besides, she knows well enough that there was never much danger to be apprehended from this ill-concerted treason; and the contempt with which she treated it will convince other discontented persons that she is not easily to be taken by surprise."

"I'm afraid her Majesty will be disappointed if she expects that these proceedings will deter Neville from entering into other plots against her; he has a restless spirit, and even though banished from England, may continue a correspondence

No. 11.

with those who are willing to hazard their lives rather than witness the triumph of the reformed religion."

" He will be too narrowly watched to give him an opportunity of practising against the sovereign," answered the Earl of Danvers.

" Nay, I question much whether his malice is ever turned against myself, for his proud spirit is not likely to brook the triumph I have obtained over him."

" You mean with respect to my daughter, I suppose?"

" I do : his ambitious views have been foiled, and though I do not believe he ever entertained any real regard for Blanche, he will not easily forgive the man who has been the chief cause of his present disgrace."

" But," observed Sir Richard, " he will be removed far enough away from you in a short time."

" Ay," answered the earl, " but there may be those left behind, who will undertake to execute any design that he may have in view against me; not that I feel much apprehension of his succeeding in his plots, though it will require all my watchfulness and care to guard myself from any treacherous attack that may be made against my life."

" Do you apprehend, then, that he would proceed to such an extremity?"

" It is merely a suspicion," replied the nobleman; " but from former experience of the bitterness of his hatred, I have no doubt that such a notion will enter his brains. At all events, Sir Richard, it will be only an act of prudence to be on my guard, so as to frustrate any scheme that he may form to rid himself of a rival that he regards with so much ill-feeling."

" And have not I also reason to apprehend evil from him?" demanded the baronet. " Does he not throw all the blame of his disappointment upon me; and may not one of his first acts be to wreak his vengeance upon the father of the mistress he has lost in a manner so sudden and unexpected?"

" There is, indeed, reason to apprehend his violence," answered the Earl of Danvers, " but whilst keeping a watch over him for myself, I shall not be unmindful of your safety. Besides, he may not have given up all thought of obtaining the hand of your daughter, and in that case he will rather court your friendship than commit an act that must for ever end all his hopes of obtaining the rich dowry he expected to receive with Blanche."

" I rather think he has abandoned all expectation of that kind," replied the other, " for I observed the look with which he regarded her when he left the room, and from the terrible expression of his countenance it seemed to me that hatred had succeeded the love he once possessed towards her."

" Do you think he meditates mischief against your daughter?"

" I fear so ; but of course I have no very positive ground for the opinion I have formed."

" You have awakened my suspicion upon that point," said the earl, " and I shall not rest satisfied till I have ascertained whether your notion is well founded. That Henry Neville is the slave of evil passions, I know, but I can hardly persuade myself that he would seek to injure a woman for no other reason than that she has preferred another."

" But he is unused to be foiled," exclaimed Sir Richard; " and having but little control over his passions, it is not unlikely that he may form some desperate design to revenge himself for the disappointment he has been compelled to suffer."

" Then I will plainly question him upon the subject," cried the earl, " and demand an equally plain answer ere I leave him."

" My lord, it would be madness to seek an interview with him under his present state of excitement."

" Nay," answered the Earl of Danvers, " he knows I am a match for him in swordsmanship, and his violence will not be so easily excited as you imagine. Be that as it may, however, I will seek him out and demand a reply to my questions."

The nobleman was heedless of all remonstrance, and leaving Blanche in the care of her father he strode away in search of his incensed and disappointed rival.

CHAPTER XI.

Art thou so lost to every sense of shame
And honour? Hast thou no manhood in thee
That thou canst malice bear against a girl
Whose hand thou once didst seek?—ESTEVAN.

POOR Nicodemus Dove was in a terrible panic when he observed the fierce looks of Neville as he left the room, and afterwards, when he also quitted the Hall, he looked about in every direction in the hope of finding the young man and remonstrating with him upon entertaining an ill feeling against his rival, when he had so short a time to make preparations for leaving England. Luckily for him, however, he did not succeed in finding the object of his search till the rage of Henry Neville had somewhat cooled; and as the poet also had had time for reflection, he approached the subject he had in his mind with some little caution. It was in the garden that he found Henry Neville, who was pacing rapidly up and down one of the walks, and meditating upon the events which had occurred to him within the last hour. At first Nicodemus felt a great inclination to retrace his steps, but upon second thoughts he determined to carry out his design, and, presenting himself before the young man, demanded with a smiling countenance if he might be allowed to inquire the subject of his meditations.

"Why dost thou ask me, sirrah?" exclaimed Henry Neville, suddenly stopping short, and fixing his eyes upon the countenance of the querist as if he would look him through. "But I see how it is," he added after a pause—"thou hast been sent to torment me because my enemies are not yet satisfied with the triumph they have just obtained over me."

"Upon my life, Master Neville," answered the poet, "you are very much out there, for my coming to look after you was quite a voluntary act; and, as for Sir Richard Langdale and the earl, I left them both together, talking, I suppose, about the marriage of Miss Blanche and—"

"Would you drive me mad by speaking upon that subject?" cried the young man, interrupting him, and raising his arm as if to grasp him by the throat. But Nicodemus foresaw what was coming, and being gifted with a tolerable share of agility, he skipped on one side, and thus in all probability escaped a squeeze that would for ever have deprived the world of one of its poets.

"Master Neville," he exclaimed, "this rage of yours is most unseemly, seeing that I come here as a friend and not as an enemy. I would give you the benefit, and you repay my intended kindness by attempting to take my life."

"I want not such advice as thou canst give," answered Neville, in a tone of despondency.

"How know you that, when you have not yet heard what I have to say?" demanded the other. "I thought you appeared to be in a great deal of trouble, and, like a fool as I am, I intend to give you the benefit and advantage of my counsel."

"Will your counsel restore me to the same position in which I stood but a short time since?"

"No, it won't do that, certainly," answered Nicodemus; "but I had a notice that you intended to challenge this outlaw—or earl—or whatever he is, and if that had been the case, I should have warned you to have nothing to do with him."

"Why?"

"Simply because you are no fair match for him."

"You think, then, that his power with the sword is superior to my own?"

"I have no doubt about it," replied Nicodemus, "and, if I am not mistaken, you have had proof of it before now."

"It must be admitted that I have crossed swords with him," said Henry Neville, "and he had the presumption to claim the advantage, though I had as much right to it as he had. Indeed, if it had not been for the assistance afforded him by that hag, Dame Dagley, he would not have been alive this day to exult in the fall of his rival for the hand of Blanche Langdale."

"Then, Dame Dagley lies most confoundedly," exclaimed Nicodemus, "for she declares that the advantage was all on his side, and that you had not a chance with him from first to last."

"To whom did she say so?"

"Oh, to a great many other persons besides myself."

"Indeed'!—she has been at some pains, then, in her attempt to blast my character?"

"I don't know how that may be," replied the poet; "but people are pretty much inclined to believe her, though I have been at some pains to convince them that the advantage was all on your own side. And as for her being your enemy, Master Neville, it is not much to be wondered at, I think, seeing that you set fire to her cottage a short time ago, and she and her family would have been houseless if Sir Richard had not put them into another."

"I would that she and all who belong to her had perished in the flames," muttered Neville, through his clenched teeth.

"There is little reason to wish that," observed the other, "for if any of them had been killed, you would have stood a fair chance of being tried for their murder. Indeed, even as it is, a man of less standing in the world than yourself would have got into trouble for burning the poor devils out of house and home."

"Psha! when does the world ever heed what becomes of such low-born slaves as these Dagleys?"

"That's very true," answered Nicodemus, "but it's a shame, though, that there should not be as much protection for the poor as for the rich. I have often thought of writing a poem upon the subject, the first few lines of which, with your permission, I'll now repeat."

"You will please to do no such thing, for I am in no humour to encourage your foolery."

"Foolery, Master Neville!"

"Ay; by what milder term can I call it?"

"You might just as well have called it the inspiration of intellect," retorted Nicodemus Dove; "for I can assure you I take a great deal of pains with my verses, and it's hard to be told after all that they are nothing more than foolery."

"Then, all I ask of you is never to inflict any of your so-called poetry upon me," exclaimed Henry Neville. "At no time am I very partial to jingling rhymes, but they are doubly annoying to me, now that I have other matters of more importance to think of."

"What! you prefer, then, brooding over the quarrel that has taken place between you and the chap we used to call the Outlaw?"

"If I brood over it," answered Neville, "it is in the hope that the hour is not far off when I shall have an opportunity to revenge the wrongs he has done met. I writhe under the infliction, and when once I feel myself aggrieved, I never rest till the insult has been washed out by the blood of my enemy."

"And yet, between ourselves, Master Neville," observed the poet, "it strikes me very forcibly that the Earl of Danvers has quite as much to complain of as you have."

"How can that be, when he exults in having deprived me of the hand of Blanche Langdale?"

"I know nothing about the young lady's hand," replied Nicodemus Dove, "but recent events proved clearly enough that she never gave you her heart."

"I care not about her loving me so that she becomes my wife."

"Then she has shown her good sense in refusing your offer. She knew, I suppose, that there was no chance of happiness for her, and preferring your rival, she was not to blame for accepting his offer instead of yours."

"She will see a little reason to repent it, though," muttered Henry Neville, "for though my time is short in England, I will not quit my native shores, till I have either revenged my wrongs, or at least, made an attempt to do so."

"There are you wrong, then, my good sir."

" Can you tell me in what respect I am wrong ?"

" To be sure, I can," answered Nicodemus ; " you have been lucky to get off so easily, when the queen might have sent you to the Tower of London, and if I was in your place, I would get away from this country as quickly as possible, for fear she should happen to take it into her head to change her mind."

" Let her send me to the scaffold, if she pleases," returned the other, gloomily, " for blasted as my prospects are, I care not how soon, nor by what means, my life is brought to a close."

" So I should imagine by your going on at such a head-strong pace," exclaimed Nicodemus Dove. " Here's as pretty an opportunity to make yourself comfortable as any man need wish for, and yet you must needs throw away all your chances for the sake of revenging yourself upon a man that you never met till very lately."

" Humph ! and so it has come to this, that I must be schooled and lectured by an idiot."

" Not so much of an idiot, Master Neville, as you may think for," retorted the other, indignantly. " I may sometimes speak and write in a style of language that exceeds your comprehension to understand ; but there are other people in the world—ay, and a good many of 'em, too, who can see, not only that I write good poetry, but that I shall by-and-by be immortalised by the productions of my pen."

" In that case," answered Henry Neville, " there must be more fools in the world than I thought for. However, be that as it may, I am in no humour to endure this intrusion of yours any longer. Begone ! or I may be guilty of an act of violence towards you that I shall afterwards regret."

" Begone !" exclaimed Nicodemus ; " am I not a visitor of Sir Richard Langdale, and haven't I as much right to take a walk in his garden as you have ?"

" Granted, but I must request you to enjoy the gratification by yourself. There are other walks here Master Dove, besides this one, and you have, therefore, no excuse for forcing yourself any longer upon my society."

" But suppose I prefer this one ?"

" Why, then, we must e'en cross swords upon the matter," exclaimed Neville ; and, drawing his weapon as he spoke, he threw himself back a couple of paces, as if preparing to commence an assault. This, however, was going further than had ever entered the contemplation of the poet, and, drawing his cloak about him, he immediately commenced a precipitate retreat towards the house, near which he was met by the Earl of Danvers, who was still prosecuting his search after his rival. Nicodemus then began to think he was safe, and disguising his alarm as well as he could, he strutted up to the nobleman, saluted him in passing, and was making his way towards the hall of entrance, when the earl inquired of him if he had chanced to see Neville in the course of his ramble."

" Seen him !" echoed the poet ; " I rather think I have, too ; and I fancy the young gentleman won't forget in a hurry the interview that he and I have had together."

" Indeed ! have there been words between you ?"

" Ay, and very angry ones too."

" How did they arrise ?"

" Through my good nature," answered Nicodemus. " I tried to make peace between you and him, and the end of it was, that my sword was drawn from its scabbard, and——"

" Why, surely you were not engaged in a duel on my account ?" interrupted the earl.

" Not exactly," replied Nicodemus, " but it came pretty near to one though. I have always courage enough to defend myself in cases of need, and if Master Neville had only been of my way of thinking, either his life or mine would have been sacrificed."

" I'm afraid, then," observed his lordship, smiling, "that in this instance at least your courage had almost exceeded your discretion."

" Why, the truth of it is, my lord," answered Nicodemus, pompously, " any one who calls himself a man won't allow himself to be insulted, without taking steps to protect his honour. Now, Henry Neville has insulted me, and therefore you can feel little surprise at my calling him to account for it."

" And all this arose from something that he said about me ?"

"Partly from that cause, and partly from another," replied the poet. " The long and the short of it is, that he spoke disparagingly of my writings, and if that won't stir up a man's wrath, I don't know what will."

" Perhaps, he gave his opinion honestly."

" That may be, my lord, but it was none the more pleasant on that account, and the honesty of Mr. Neville might have cost him his life, if it had not been that his prudence taught him discretion."

" Can it be possible that he refused your challenge ?"

" Ay, and for once in his life he acted wisely. But what, my lord, makes you think he would not refuse to fight me ?"

" Because, from what I have seen of Henry Neville, he has always been rash and impetuous in a quarrel. I have myself met him as a foe, and, to speak candidly of him, I never thought that cowardice was among his failings."

" It seems, then, you don't altogether believe what I have been telling you, my lord ?"

" I will not go so far as to say that," answered the earl; " but you are an author, Master Dove, and being accustomed to make use of a poetic licence, I thought it possible you might have exaggerated a little in the present instance. But I cry your pardon, my dear sir ; enough has been already said upon this subject, and we will therefore, with your leave, say no more about it. Perhaps, you will have the goodness to direct me to the spot where I may find Mr. Neville."

" I have no objection to do so, on one condition."

" Well, sir, and what is the condition ?"

" That you don't get into a quarrel with him."

" You are afraid, then, I suppose, that if swords were drawn, I should get the worst of it ?"

" To tell you the truth, my lord, that's just what I am afraid of," answered Nicodemus.

" And yet it appears you think yourself a match for him ?"

" Nay," answered the poet, " I am not much given to vain boasting, but the truth is, I am not an unskilful swordsman, neither do I lack courage when I know my cause is a just one."

" But it appears that you think I do."

" On the contrary," returned Nicodemus, " I know you to be brave, though withal a little too hot-headed to be upon your guard with an experienced fencer like Master Henry Neville. Besides, he bears you the most deadly hatred, and if once you meet together in strife, he'll never give in till either you or he have got your death wound."

" Be that as it may, we shall meet with equal chances," answered the Earl of Danvers. " If he is rash and impetuous, as you say, therein lies a better chance that I may have the advantage of him ; but whether or not, he shall find that he has an honourable antagonist to deal with. So now direct me where to find him, for if this quarrel of ours is to come to a bloody issue, the sooner it is over, the better."

" Don't you think, my lord, it would be a wiser plan to leave it till another day ?"

" I ask not your advice, neither am I inclined to receive it," exclaimed the Earl of Danvers. " You have been asked a question, and if it is not quickly replied to, I shall leave you and go in search of my enemy."

" Oh, if that's the case, I may as well tell you at once," said Nicodemus, evidently very unwilling to afford the information he had been asked for. " You will find him in yonder path that skirts the lawn ; and if fighting is really intended, I know of no better place for it than the green sward."

Before Nicodemus Dove had finished, however, the earl darted from him with the speed of lightning, taking the direction which had been pointed out to him

To offer any further advice or opposition would, therefore, be in vain ; and, as one way only remained to prevent hostilities taking place, he made the best of his way into the house, to apprise Sir Richard Langdale of what was going on, and thus obtain the necessary assistance to prevent the mischief that might be anticipated. But, unfortunately, the baronet was not to be found, so that Nicodemus had to wander from place to place before he could obtain any clue to the person he was in search of.

In the meantime, the earl made his way towards the spot where he had been told he should meet Henry Neville, but on arriving there, he found, to his disappointment and chagrin, that his rival was no longer there. In a few seconds, however, footsteps were heard close at hand, and, looking round him, he observed Neville advancing from a shrubbery with which that part of the garden was bounded. The glaring eyes of the young man plainly announced the feeling of satisfaction with which he observed the presence of his rival, and having advanced to within three or four paces, he demanded if the interview had occurred through chance or design.

"From design, most assuredly," answered the nobleman. "I heard that you were to be found in this spot, and immediately hastened hither to learn from your own lips whether I am henceforth to regard you as a friend or an enemy."

"There could be little need to ask me such a question," returned the other, haughtily, "for, after what has occurred this day, you may be well assured that I can never regard you in any other light than as my sworn foe."

"And yet," exclaimed the nobleman, "I must confess my ignorance as to what has caused this ill-feeling."

"Indeed! Is it nothing, think you, to rob a man of the mistress of his affections?"

"Really, sir," answered the earl, "I know not of any act of mine that can justify the harsh words you have applied to me."

"Then that," exclaimed Henry Neville, "must be because you are mean-spirited enough to be afraid of the man whose anger you have kindled."

"Hear me, Master Neville," cried the other, becoming somewhat excited by this taunt; "you have been pleased to utter things which one man of honour has no right to say to another. I have hitherto managed to control my passion, but where a deliberate insult is offered I will draw my sword in my own defence, even though it be within the hospitable domains of Sir Richard Langdale.

"Why, that is the very point I wanted to come at," retorted the other. "I have received orders to quit England within a certain limited period, and it is my determination not to go into banishment till I have called you to an account for certain injuries that I have received at your hands."

"You shall not hear me refuse any call that may be made upon me," answered the Earl of Danvers, "but I must first know that there are grounds sufficient to warrant me in accepting your challenge."

"Have I not said that you have robbed me of my mistress ?"

"You have said so," replied the nobleman, "but I most positively deny the truth of your charge. Blanche Langdale was secretly pledged to me long ere her acquaintance with you commenced, and it is I, therefore, who have most reason to complain of the pertinacity with which your suit was pressed."

"I wooed her with the consent of her father."

"And how was that consent obtained ?" demanded the earl. "You prevailed upon him to join in a conspiracy that had nearly ended in his ruin, and it was in consequence of the high hopes you held out to him that he was induced to promise you the hand of his daughter. Luckily the plot was discovered in good time, and to that fact alone does the baronet owe the clemency which has been extended towards him by the queen."

"And you, I suppose, are the informer to whom we owe the frustration of our plans."

"I confess that it was partly through me the plot was discovered," answered the nobleman. "The presence of Arnheim and the priest first awakened my suspicions that foul play was going on, and subsequent observations confirmed me in the opinion I had formed. Duty to my sovereign demanded that I should warn her of the danger with which she was threatened, and I lost no time in doing so, though under a promise that the guilty parties should suffer no very severe punishment. You have now all the facts of the case before you, and it now only remains to say whether, as a loyal subject, I have exceeded my duty."

"It's easy enough to find excuses even for the basest conduct," exclaimed Henry Neville, "and the explanation you have given removes none of the odium that attaches itself to those who act the dishonoured part of a spy. For the failure of the plot I care not, but it is not so easy to forget that it is to you I owe the loss of Blanche Langdale."

"Blanche never loved you," replied the earl, "and to my own certain knowledge she was resolved never to become your wife, even though by the refusal she might bring upon herself the everlasting anger of her parent."

"So the girl might vaunt to you," exclaimed Henry Neville, "but her refusal would have been of but little avail when her father was resolved upon the marriage, even though her obstinacy should force him to drag her to the altar."

"And would you have made her your wife under such circumstances of cruelty and oppression?"

"Why should I hesitate," demanded Neville, "when all other hope had failed me?"

"Because you never entertained any real regard for her."

"So you are pleased to say," replied the other, "but I deny the truth of your assertion. I loved the girl, and but for you, I should, ere many days, have been her husband."

"Ay," answered the earl, "you would have obtained the casket, but not the jewel it should have contained. Blanche Langdale might have been forced to become your bride, but her love you never would have had."

"And if so," exclaimed Neville, gloomily, "who should I have had to thank for her coldness but you? You have been my bane, my curse, and, in exchange for it, I heap upon you my everlasting curses."

"Your curses, Master Neville, will never harm me."

"No, but my sword may."

"That will depend upon which of us can make the best use of our swords."

"Then, let us bring the point to an issue at once," exclaimed Henry Neville, throwing himself into an attitude of defence.

"What!" cried the earl, "when we are so near the house, that the clashing of our weapons will be certain to be heard."

"Then, go with me into yonder meadow, where before assistance can arrive, our quarrel will be brought to an end."

"There are reasons," answered the Earl of Danvers, "why I am resolved not to comply with your demand. One of them, and that not the least, is, that I would not abuse the hospitality of Sir Richard Langdale by making any part of his domain the scene of our conflict."

"Then to your teeth, I pronounce you to be a coward, and unworthy the knighthood that has been conferred upon you."

And so saying, he aimed a blow at the earl, which doubtless would have proved mortal, had he not been so well prepared as to be able to parry it, and then to throw himself into an attitude of defence. Even the Earl of Danvers had by this time become excited, and the quick clashing of their swords showed the earnest determination with which both of them had entered into the conflict. In point of skill, there seemed to be but little difference, and the issue of the combat was still uncertain, when loud voices were heard, and Sir Richard Langdale, followed by Nicodemus Dove, and several of his retainers were seen approaching at their utmost speed. This at once brought the strife to a close, and sheathing his weapon, Henry Neville turned away, muttering as he did so, that he would again seek his rival ere the expiration of many hours.

Scarcely had he taken his departure, when the baronet, and those by whom he was accompanied, reached the spot where the Earl of Danvers was standing.

"What is the meaning of all this?" exclaimed Sir Richard; "methinks, my lord, if you must indulge in fighting and brawling, you might have found a more suitable place than the garden of your host."

"I merit your reproach," answered the nobleman, "and yet, goaded as I was by the words of yonder madman, it is little to be marvelled at that I was at length urged to draw my sword against him."

"Well, well," exclaimed the old baronet, "if the fault was not yours, I will no longer reproach you for what has occurred. And for once in his life Nicodemus Dove has done us good service, for, except through the information he brought me, this affray would have ended only in the loss of a life."

"Yes," cried the poet, not a little flattered by this compliment, "it was I who

No. 12

old Sir Richard what was going on, and trouble enough I had to find him, too, but knowing the danger of delay, I hunted about the premises, and met with him just in time to put an end to the mischief that was likely to happen."

" You have acted with more than your usual discrimination," observed the baronet, " and I shall with much pleasure take an early opportunity to return the obligation you have placed me under."

" Am I at liberty to urge the only favour I have to ask ?" demanded Nicodemus Dove.

" Certainly."

" Then it is that you will bestow upon me your youngest daughter in marriage."

" That, my dear sir," answered the old man, " is a subject which we cannot discuss at the present moment. Indeed, upon the least reflection, you must be aware that my daughter has some right to be consulted in an affair which so nearly concerns her own future happiness."

" No doubt of it, Sir Richard," exclaimed the other, " but I can't forget that a few hours since you were determined to marry your other daughter to a man she didn't love."

" True," returned the baronet, " but recent events have served to convince me of the injustice I had almost been guilty of. I have now given you my answer, and having none other to give at present, you will perhaps allow me, without further interruption, to ask a question or two of the Earl of Danvers."

" I beg your pardon, Sir Richard," persisted the poet, " but I should really like to know whether there is any chance of my being made happy with the hand of Miss Catherine Langdale ?"

" And I," returned Sir Richard, " must be excused giving any other answer than that which you have already received. My daughter must first be consulted, and if she has no objection to the marriage you are so anxious for, I promise that on my part there shall be no opposition offered to it." Then addressing himself to the nobleman, he continued—"At present, my lord, I have received no explanation of the origin of the quarrel that had like to have ended so disastrously: may I ask if it arose from disappointment on the part of your rival at seeing Blanche likely to become the bride of another ?"

" Your guess is not very wide of the mark," answered the earl, " but the affair is of so little consequence that I would rather the subject of our quarrel was not again mentioned. It is sufficient for me that I have been promised my long-sought prize, and if Henry Neville has any further difference to settle, he knows where to find me, and may rest assured that I shall not meanly endeavour to avoid him."

" What! are you still inclined to carry on this quarrel till it comes to a fatal issue ?"

" I have no other alternative left, if he persists in bringing matters to such a climax."

" Well, well," observed Sir Richard, after a brief reflection, " there is some consolation in knowing that in a short time you will both be separated widely enough asunder. He dare not refuse to obey the queen's orders to depart the kingdom within fourteen days, and when once he is gone, you may hope to marry Blanche without a chance of further interruption."

" That is to say if he leaves no emissaries behind him to execute any act of vengeance that he may have formed."

" Emissaries !" exclaimed the baronet ; " think you, then, Henry Neville would be base enough to employ others to perform such an act of villany as you have spoken of?"

" I have yet seen no reason to think otherwise of him," replied the Earl of Danvers, " and from the experience I have had, there is sufficient ground to believe that he can possess but small claim to any feeling of honour. Nay, even within this last half hour he would have slain me upon this very spot had I not in some respect been prepared for an act of treachery."

" The more reason that you should avoid him."

" Avoid him ! and is it you, Sir Richard Langdale, who would advise me to be guilty of an act of cowardice ?"

" The truth is, I have learned something from experience," answered the baronet, " and it has taught me that prudence is not always deemed cowardice by the more sensible portion of the world. Besides, you seem altogether to have forgotten the alarm this quarrel will occasion my daughter, who even now is awaiting our return with anxiety and suspense.

" Humph ! Was Nicodemus Dove so thoughtless, then, as to tell her what had occurred ?"

" How could I help letting the cat out of the bag, when she was the first person I happened to meet with ?" demanded the poet. " The young lady saw by my trepidation that there was something in the wind, and I couldn't tell her a lie when the question was fairly put to me."

" But you might have abstained from letting her know that I was engaged in mortal conflict with her persecutor."

" My lord," answered Nicodemus, " it's all very easy to say what might or might not have been done, but when once a woman is determined to find out a secret, she'll never desist till all the facts have been laid open to her. Besides, I was in a hurry to find Sir Richard, and the truth popped out in order that I might encounter no further delay in searching after him."

" And don't you think," asked the baronet, " that it would have been better to interpose between the combatants, than to run away and leave them to fight it out ?"

" As for running away," answered the other, pettishly, " I've about as much courage in these sort of matters as most other people, and my only motive for going in search of you was, that I thought two of us would be more likely to disarm them than one would have been."

" Did you tell my daughter that they had drawn their swords against each other ?"

" No. I only said I was afraid there might be mischief between them if something wasn't done to prevent it."

" Knows she the place of their meeting ?"

" From me she has heard nothing more than I have informed you of," answered Nicodemus, " though it's likely enough she may have taken the trouble to watch where you and I came to."

" In that case, she will be here anon," said the baronet, addressing himself to the Earl of Danvers. " Her fears are the more likely to be excited by the mystery our friend has thought proper to observe, and should she, on her way hither, be met by Henry Neville, I am not sure that he will not endeavour to carry her off."

" He dare not make such an attempt," exclaimed the nobleman, fiercely, " for experience has taught him that my wrath is not to be kindled with impunity, and were he to offer such an act of violence to Blanche Langdale, I would pursue him with my vengeance even to the farthest extremity of the earth."

" I know your courage, my lord," answered the baronet, " and am well convinced that you would revenge any insult that might be offered to my daughter. On the other hand, however, I am most anxious to prevent another meeting between such fiery spirits and you will therefore oblige me by avoiding Henry Neville, rather than risk your life in an encounter with him."

" Ay," retorted the earl, " and thus give him an opportunity of branding me with the name of coward."

" Psha!—who would believe such an accusation ?"

" There are persons," replied the nobleman, " who would not only believe it, but rejoice at having some excuse to ruin my character in the estimation of the wo rld.'

"Then," said the poet, "I should tell them,—

> To mind their own business,
> Lest slanderous words
> Should provoke me to meet them
> With pistols or swords.
> And should that not be heeded,
> I'd——"

"Hush!" interrupted Sir Richard Langdale, "the remainder of your effusion must be finished some other time, for yonder I see my daughter approaching us, and we must be prepared to allay her apprehensions by the best ex s we can invent. So let us go to meet her, my lord, and of all things let there be nothing in your words or manner to confirm the alarm that she may be under with regard to your safety."

He then took the earl's arm, and led him towards Blanche, who, by that time, had nearly reached the spot where they were standing. The poet, who was not best pleased at the interruption he had met with, turned off in another direction grumbling and discontented.

CHAPTER XII.

> Thou dost not know me yet,
> For I am one of those whose will is law,
> And he who baulks it is an enemy
> I never can forgive.—THE WARDEN.

WHEN Stephen Dagley and his dame returned to their cottage, they found their daughter Martha anxiously awaiting their arrival, for she had seen Neville loitering about the place, and knowing his ungovernable disposition she felt apprehensive lest some fresh violence was meditated. And even when their rap was heard, she hesitated to open the door, till the well-known tone of her father's voice assured her that her fears were groundless, and that those who had applied for admittance were the friends from whom alone she could hope for protection against the violence she dreaded ; at length with a trembling hand the fastenings were removed and her parents entered the cottage.

"Why, what ails thee, now, wench," exclaimed Stephen, as he observed the trepidation of his daughter ; "what has happened to thee, Martha, that thou must needs shake and tremble like an aspen leaf?"

"I am ashamed to say that I have been alarmed without sufficient cause," replied the girl; "and yet I can never see him without feeling that I am in danger."

"Him!" exclaimed Stephen; "who is the girl talking about?"

"I spoke of Master Henry Neville."

"Psha!—he is at Holmwood Castle."

"How long is it since you saw him there ?"

"Humph!—about an hour ago."

"Then, he has been here since then," answered Martha, "and I fear for no good purpose."

"You'll think differently when you know all that has taken place lately," exclaimed Stephen, "for the serpent has been deprived of his sting, and what's more, he'll have to leave England within fourteen days, or he and the scaffold will have a chance of being better acquainted."

"That, dear father, is, indeed, good news," cried Martha, suddenly rousing herself from the despondency into which she had fallen.

"Ay," interposed the dame, "and it is not the only good news we have brought thee, my girl. We have to tell thee something of the Outlaw, who, instead of being a fugitive from justice, turns out to have been a great lord in disguise."

"A great lord!" cried Martha with surprise; "then he must have had a reason for coming to hide himself in this wild forest of ours."

"To be sure he had," answered her father; "he was in love with Blanche Langdale, but, as there was a quarrel between his family and hers, he was obliged to come here under an assumed character, in order to prevent a discovery taking place till after a reconciliation had been effected."

"Then," sighed the girl, "he will be too proud and too great ever to visit us again."

"I don't know how that may be," answered Stephen Dagley, "but I should suppose it will make very little difference to you whether he ever comes again or not. The Earl of Danvers has never cast a thought upon the daughter of a humble woodman, or, if he has, it could only have been to bring shame and dishonour upon her."

"Nay, you wrong him there, father," cried Martha, warmly, "for never has he uttered a word that might not as well have been pronounced in your own hearing. He has always been to me as a brother, and if I feel sorry at the discovery that has taken place, it is that we shall no longer see him here as we were wont to do when he was known only as an Outlaw."

"You think then," exclaimed Dame Dagley, "that he will not be grateful for the favours we have done him."

"Ingratitude, I believe, he never can be guilty of," answered the maiden, timidly; "but it seems he is likely to marry Blanche Langdale, and when she becomes his wife, he will take her far from home, and it is likely we shall never again hear of him."

"And what matters it if we do not?" demanded her father. "He has never been aught to us but a stranger whom we have taken some interest in, when we believed that he needed our assistance, and to speak my mind, girl, I shall not be sorry at his leaving this neighbourhood, since there will at length be some chance of your accepting the offer of Arnold Brockhurst, who has long sought thy hand, with little chance of gaining while there was a rival in his way."

"The supposed Outlaw was never his rival," answered Martha, "for I always knew that his heart was given to another."

"Do you mean to tell me, then, that you never indulged a thought of becoming his wife?"

"Never."

"Humph!—that is rather strange too, considering the frequent secret meetings you have had with him."

"They appear not to have been very secret," she replied, "since you have known of them."

"Yes, Martha, I knew of them," he exclaimed, "and it must be confessed I at one time trembled for your safety when I found that you gave so much of your confidence to a perfect stranger. I, however, resolved to keep a close watch upon both of you, and 'tis well I did so, for the more I saw of the stranger the less cause did I see to fear that any treachery was plotting against your happiness."

"You saw that he regarded me as a sister?"

"I did."

"And what is more," added the dame, "I myself very lately took an opportunity to speak to him upon the subject."

"And you were satisfied with his answer?"

"Perfectly so," replied the dame, "and it was well that he could so thoroughly clear up the doubts that began to enter my brain; for had he failed to do so, I would have revenged myself in such a manner that he should never again have had a chance of practising against the confidence of an unsuspecting girl."

"I understand," cried Martha Dagley, "believing him to be a fugitive from justice, you would have surrendered him to those that you thought were his enemies."

"There you are wrong," answered her mother, "for I always knew that he was not what had been represented, though till within these last two hours I suspected not the high station to which he belongs. My opinion was that he was a victim of persecution, and he was welcome to such protection as we had power to give, but had he proved ungrateful he should have died, even if there had been no other hand than mine to slay him !"

"And is he now safe?" demanded Martha, anxiously.

"He is."

"Have all your suspicions against him vanished?"

"Ay, girl, every one of them," answered her mother; "my own eyes have convinced me that my fears had been raised without sufficient cause, and well pleased was I to observe that the stranger had never contemplated the ingratitude I had suspected him of."

"That is to say, as far as you know of," observed Stephen Dagley, interposing; "for my own part I know not what could have brought him so often to our cottage, if it was not love for our daughter, and now that we have discovered his high rank and station, I begin to fancy he must have had a notion that it would be no difficult matter to betray the daughter of people as humble as ourselves."

"Then you believe him to be a villain?" said Martha Dagley, in accents of indignation.

"Why, as for that," replied her father, "it was not much to be wondered at if my suspicions were roused, seeing that he was a stranger to us, and there was a good deal of mystery that none of us could ever make out. Your brother Martin, too, was not without a notion of the same sort, and often have I heard him mutter vengeance, should chance ever lead to the discovery that the stranger meditated an act of treachery towards those who had afforded him shelter when most he seemed to need it."

"Yet Martin, I should suppose, will now acknowledge that his fears were groundless."

"He has already done so," answered her father, "and should an opportunity ever present itself, he will not fail to confess that he wronged the stranger by his suspicions."

"There will be little chance of his doing that, I fancy," observed Dame Dagley, "for I suppose his marriage with Blanche Langdale will not be delayed any long time; and, as soon as he becomes her husband, he will, I dare say, take her to his noble castle that I hear he has somewhere in the north of England."

"That," exclaimed Stephen, "will of course depend upon the course that Henry Neville intends to take : he may not choose to leave England, though commanded to do so by the queen, and if he remains beyond the time that has been named, we may pretty well guess that he delays his departure only till he has fulfilled some plot that he has formed."

"But her majesty," observed the dame, "is not one who will suffer an act of disobedience without punishing, and that too most severely, the person who is guilty of it."

"True," answered her husband "and yet you know as well as I do that a person might remain in this forest of ours for years without a chance of being discovered."

"Yes," responded Dame Dagley, "but that would depend upon whether he had friends in the place to assist in concealing him. Now we have never seen reason to form much of an attachment towards Henry Neville, and the chances are that we should be the first to point out to his pursuers the places where he is most likely to be found."

"At any rate it is as well to know who are our friends and who are our enemies," exclaimed Henry Neville, suddenly presenting himself before them ; "you have spoken your minds with more freedom than if it had been known that I was so near, and I now feel perfectly well convinced that here, at least, I am looked upon as a wretch who is not worthy of compassion."

"It seems, sir," cried Stephen Dagley, bitterly, "that you have been mean enough to listen to a conversation that was never intended to reach your ears."

"There's no denying that I have overheard much of what has passed," answered Neville, "and yet there is nothing in it very surprising when it is remembered that the subject of your conversation nearly concerned myself."

"You have learned then," observed the dame, "that we suspect you have an evil esign against our daughter?"

"I gathered as much from what has passed between you and your husband," answered Neville, "and it is not very wonderful that I stepped forward to vindicate my actions. Your daughter, I believe, has no complaint to bring against me; and as that is the case, I make bold to request shelter here during the short time that I am permitted to remain in England."

"May I ask, sir," demanded the woodman, "why you seek a lodging in this place when there are so many other cottages scattered about in different parts of the forest?"

"Because I know nothing of any other person besides yourself;" he replied. "Besides, I have seen your hospitality to my rival, and surely it is not too much to ask for the same shelter that you afforded to him."

"Have you so soon forgotten," asked Dame Dagley, "that it was your hand that fired our cottage and drove us to take shelter in the miserable hovel that you would now share with us?"

"And are you so revengeful," retorted the other, "that you must needs reproach me with an act that was committed at a moment when the heat of passion had deprived me of all power and control over my own actions?"

"We have reason enough for remembering it," exclaimed Stephen Dagley, "for that cottage was as dear to us as is the mansion to its lordly possessor. I was born beneath its roof; it was the first and only house of my wife during the five-and-twenty years that we have been married, and there we thought to end our days in peace and comfort. You, however, have driven us from it, yet would now ask us to take you in here, though I believe you have urged the request for no other purpose than that you may be the better able to carry on the infamous design you have formed against the honour and happiness of my daughter."

"Fool!" muttered the libertine, "what project is it likely I can have formed when I am ordered to quit my native country within the brief period of fourteen days?"

"Aye, the time is indeed short," answered Stephen Dagley; "but, fiend-like, you would like to commit as much injury as possible even in that brief period."

"Even admitting that to be the fact," exclaimed Henry Neville, "I should play a higher game than that you have accused me of."

"That I deny," replied Dagley, "for those who would once have been proud of your society will never more permit you to associate either with themselves or their families. To your face then, Master Henry Neville, I declare that you never, with my will or consent, shall ever set foot within this door again."

"Nonsense; of what use would resistance be if I resolved to fix my abode here till the time comes when I must go into exile?"

"There are other persons who have more right to claim the honour of a visit than I can pretend to," answered the woodman.

"And who are those other persons?"

"In the first place, there is your father, whom it is most likely you will never see again."

"My father will not grieve much, even if your prognostication should be correct," retorted Neville, "and to tell the truth, there are certain family reasons that stand in the way of my paying such a visit as you have suggested."

"Then you will find more agreeable quarters at Holmwood Castle than you can expect to meet with in this humble cottage."

"How can I go there, when my rival would be constantly before me?" demanded Henry Neville.

"There is no great difficulty about it that I can see," observed the other, "for he is now the accepted lover of Blanche Langdale ;(and as all your chances are now at an end, I should now advise you to shake hands and be friends with the earl."

"*I* be friendly with him!" exclaimed the other, scornfully. "No, no: he knows well enou h what my feelings are towards him, and scarcely an hour since we met together in deadly strife, which would most likely have terminated in my favour but for the interposition of other persons who had nothing to do with our quarrel."

"You regret, then," said Dame Dagley, reproachfully, "that you have not the murder of a fellow-creature to answer for?"

"The fellow-creature you speak of," retorted Neville, "was my unsuccessful rival, and therefore my enemy,—for he deprived me of the prize I sought for; and though the interval between the present time and that of my banishment is brief, I will not leave England till I have had my revenge."

"Beware how you provoke a quarrel that may not terminate in your own favour," cried the dame.

"Humph! you think him more than a match for me then?"

"If former experience may be relied on," answered the woman, "I should say that your chances against the Earl of Danvers are small indeed. You have already had two or three encounters with him, and each time he has proved himself the better swordsman."

"'Tis false," exclaimed Neville, fiercely,—"the advantage was as much in my favour as in his, and he would have perished ere this if it had not been for your interposition when you saw that he was about to fall beneath my sword."

"Yes," she replied; "I have fortunately been the means of saving him, and frustrating the evil designs of his foe."

"And he must feel honoured," exclaimed Neville with a sneer, "at being indebted to a woman for his life."

"I should not have interfered," answered the dame, "but that I saw you had taken him at a disadvantage, and that his chances were therefore against him. Had the combat been fair, you might have fought it out for me, because I know he has both skill and courage enough to defend himself against a foe."

"Upon my life," exclaimed the other, "this wandering nobleman seems to have established himself here as a great favourite."

"And if he has," interfered Stephen Dagley, "it is because he has always acted with courtesy and kindness. When we thought he had no other home to go to he was offered one here, and every act of his has since proved that he was not unmindful of the warm hospitality with which he was received."

"Yet it cannot be denied," exclaimed the other, "that he came here under circumstances not very honourable to himself."

"In what way has he acted with dishonour?"

"Were I to enter upon that subject it would take longer time than I have to spare," answered Neville. "There is one thing, however, I have to state—and that is, that he has acted with meanness and dishonour in coming disguised to pay his addresses to a female whom he had been forbidden to see."

"And why should he not have acted as he did when all circumstances are fairly considered?" asked the woodman. "He knew there was a possibility of terminating the quarrel that existed between his family and that of Sir Richard Langdale : and I believe his chief motive was to prevent a marriage taking place between yourself and Blanche Langdale."

"Well," returned Henry Neville, "and having succeeded in his design, it is not much to be wondered at, if I now hold him as a foe with whom I can never be at peace."

"But the girl never loved you," observed Dame Dagley, "and therefore you can have nothing to complain of now that she is going to be married to the man of her choice."

" And a lucky thing it is for the young lady that things turn out as they do, observed Stephen Dagley.

" Ugh ! you think so, do you?"

" I do."

" Then you are a fool for your pains."

" Not so much a fool, Master Neville, as you are a villain."

" Hah!" exclaimed the person addressed, losing all power of control over himself, " am I to be bearded by a base-born hind like thee? I will not depart till I have slain thee, as a just punishment for thine audacity."

Henry Neville was almost choked with rage as he uttered these words ; and scarcely had he given them utterance, than, at a single spring, he threw himself upon the woodman, and seized him by the throat with so powerful a grasp that the other was unable either to utter a word or to offer the necessary resistance. It was in vain, too, that Dame Dagley and her daughter attempted to release

No. 13.

Stephen from the grasp of his assailant, the latter seemed determined not to be deprived of his revenge, and the probability is, that he would have been gratified to the utmost had not Martin at that moment rushed into the cottage, and with his axe uplifted above his head, threatened death to the assailant, unless he instantly relaxed his hold. Thus endangered, Neville had no alternative but to obey the command, and having quitted the throat of his antagonist, he advanced towards the door, and then turning round, exclaimed,—

"For the present I have been foiled in my revenge; but remember, Stephen Dagley, I shall not fail to punish you for this insolence."

With a scowl upon his countenance, Neville's thoughts still brooded on vengeance, not only upon the Earl of Danvers, by whom he considered he had been so greatly wronged, but also upon the queen; whom, though she had pardoned his meditated attempt upon her liberty if not her life, he could not forgive for sentencing him to leave the country in so short a period. After some consideration, he resolved to join his fellow-conspirators, Arnheim, and Father Francis, and, from their advice, determine upon the steps to be taken.

CHAPTER XIII

THE MEETING OF THE CONSPIRATORS.—THE PLOT.—THE ATTEMPT AT ASSASSINATION.—THE GERMAN.—CONCLUSION.

THE midnight hour has tolled from the turret clock of the castle of Holmwood and beneath the deep shadow of one of the buttresses that supported the oute walls, stood three figures. This trio was composed of Neville, the Jesuit, an Arnheim the German.

"Curses on Fortune, for a fickle jade!" exclaimed the latter, in a tone pos sessing little of good humour. "After all these weeks of secret working an plotting, to be thus foiled, is enough to make one forswear all the turmoils of politic life, and settle down as an honest tiller of the earth for the rest o his days."

"Ay," returned the Jesuit, with a slightly perceptible sneer on his lip, "an drink beer till thy brains are muddled, and dandle thine own or another man' children on thy knees, as all good Germans ought to do."

"Father," said the choleric German, his blood flushing his already scarle countenance, "your gown protects you, or my dagger should make you spea differently."

"Tut, tut!" interrupted Neville, "are we children, thus to quarrel amongs ourselves. Will you listen to my proposition, or are we to quit England withou striking a blow to retrieve our ill success?"

"What is it, man?" asked the German, impatiently, while Father Francis, by gesture, showed that he was awaiting what Neville had to propose.

"We have fourteen days' grace," said the latter, "and in that time much ma be done. Let us to London at once, and by a bold movement, achieve our futur fortunes. The queen visits the citizens in a few days, and will consequently b much in public. Gathering some few of our adherents, who know that our pro ceedings are sanctioned by the holy tribunal at Rome, let us even in public, if w cannot do so in private, attempt her life. If we succeed, the greater part of the populace will side with us. What say you both—does my proposition please you?

"Der teufel! you speak very plain," muttered the German, "and I hardly kno what to say to your proposition."

"Does your courage fail you, or does it but want rousing?"

"The foul fiend seize you both!" exclaimed the German, "why are you so fond of using your taunts? My courage is as warm as yours, Master Neville, an you like you can put it to the test on the moment."

" Yes, and bring the inmates of the castle about us with the noise ; that would be sensible, truly. But what are you resolved upon ?" added Neville, addressing both his conpanions. "Time flies fast, and our position is not one of the safest."

Father Francis grasped Henry Neville by the hand warmly, and said in a deep tone of full determination,—

" I am with you—to the death!"

" A thousand devils! and so am I then," said the German with a sudden energy.

After this resolution it was determined they should separate, and each make his way to London ; the place of meeting being a little inn in the neighbourhood of the Tower, known by the sign of the " Golden Crown," where measures could be taken for carrying out their base plot.

Silently now they glided from the spot, and as they did so, with minds full of the basest designs against a woman and a sovereign whose clemency they had already so deeply experienced, not one thought of remorse glided across their callous hearts—all was dark and guilty as the deed they contemplated.

* * * * * *

The disappearance of Neville and his associates from the neighbourhood of Holmwood Castle was a matter of rejoicing to those whose stream of life had been so sadly ruffled by their machinations.

Sir Richard Langdale, who was overjoyed at his liberation from the trammels of the conspiracy into which he had been rather unwillingly drawn by the wiles of Neville, felt a greater satisfaction than he chose to express when he learnt their departure, for he fully believed, with many others, that they had not chosen to avail themselves of the fourteen days' grace allowed them by the queen, but had at once quitted England ; and he was further rejoiced, because it gave him an opportunity of at once proceeding with the preparation for the celebration of his daughter's nuptials with Lord Danvers.

Blanche and her lover, happy in themselves, did not make any objection when Sir Richard insisted that an early day should be fixed for their marriage, and everyone looked forward to its arrival with the greatest anxiety and impatience.

As to Nicodemus, he was not a man to live single, and it was not long before he succeeded in winning, by the sweet persuasion of his poetic genius, a wife, whose temper was as spirited as her face was pretty, and who found but little difficulty in ruling her husband in a manner she best thought fit.

Catherine Langdale, of course, saving the bride, was the brightest beauty of the wedding ; and not many months elapsed before a gallant young knight, a friend of the Lord Danvers, and who first saw her on that auspicious day, led her forth from her father's castle, a happy bride.

Stephen Dagley and his family were generously remembered for their kindness to the noble Danvers, while he was playing the part of an outlaw in merry Sherwood Forest. Their cottage was newly erected, in a style of comfort far superior to that of former days, and Martin Dagley received permission from Sir Richard Langdale to shoot a fat buck, as often as the necessities the family might require it.

* * * * * * *

Turn we now to the three remaining characters of our tale, Neville, Arnheim, and the Jesuit, whom we left making their way with all speed towards London.

According to appointment, they met on the evening of the fourth day, at the Golden Crown, and, that no time might be lost, they instantly set about gaining intelligence as to the movements of the Queen. The host was a man of very great loquacity, and when he was invited to partake of a tankard of his own ale, and then, in a deferential tone, was asked a number of questions relative to the court, his tongue readily loosened, and all the information required by the conspirators was soon obtained.

The next was the day appointed for Elizabeth's visit to the city, and, if the attempt was to be made, it must be made then, for no other opportunity was likely to offer itself. To Arnheim was entrusted the summoning of those adherents whom they knew could be trusted, and who, being in the pay of Rome, were always prepared for such an emergency. These persons were to be posted in a body near the east end of the cathedral of St. Paul, round which the state carriage would pass, and which would be the most exposed part of the whole route. Neville and Father Francis, both armed with petronels, were to take their stand in the foremost rank of spectators, and on the arrival of the carriage at the appointed spot, both were to take aim, and fire at the Queen, Arnheim at the same moment forcing an opening through the crowd at their back, for the purpose of enabling them to effect their escape, when they were to join the more influential members of their party, who would instantly proceed to take measures for the installation of Mary Stuart on the throne of England.

These arrangements determined upon, they separated for the night, and Arnheim at once proceeded to assemble his men.

" Ha! ha !" he chuckled, as he made his way in the direction of the Tower, " my time has come now. I will be their tool no longer. When my services are wanted, all is fair words and fine phrases ; but when that time is passed, taunts, and jeers, and sneers at my country are all that are thought good for me. And Master Neville, too—we have crossed swords before now, and not without cause. Well, well, as I have said, my time is come now, and I will revenge all, save myself, and put gold in my pouch. Arnheim, the German, may be stupid and heavy-brained, but he will be a match for the wily Jesuit yet. And why should I, who sell the services of my good sword for gold, risk my life in such a service as this ?"

Thus muttering to himself, Arnheim at length reached the Tower, and asked to see the Lord Chamberlain on business of great importance.

The morning dawned upon as gay a scene as the worthy citizens of London had ever witnessed. The narrow streets soon became one living mass of human beings, and cheerfulness sat upon the features of every one present.

About an hour before the expected coming of the royal *cortege*, Neville and Father Francis took their stations in St. Paul's Churchyard. The heavy countenance of Arnheim, seen for a moment amid the crowd behind them, gave them the assurance that all was arranged, and they awaited with anxiety and impatience the arrival of the moment when they should be able to bring their plot to a consummation.

At last, loud cheering was heard in the distance ; nearer and nearer it came, until at length the proximity of the sounds told that the procession had reached the top of Ludgate-hill, where it paused or a few moments, to permit the Queen to listen to an address in Latin, spoken by one of the boys belonging to Christchurch, and also to witness a grand pageant, representing the union of Peace and Commerce, which had been prepared for her inspection.

The procession once more moved on, and as the escort slowly rode by the spot where Neville and the priest were stationed, they both cocked their petronels, and strung their nerves for the attempt, when a couple of halberds flashed before their eyes, the petronels were dashed from their hands, and the two conspirators found themselves powerless in the hands of a body of the City Guards, while, at but a few paces' distance, regarding them with a smile of triumph, was the form of Arnheim the German.

Neville and Father Francis were at once consigned to a dungeon in the Tower, and were soon brought to trial, and, after a short examination, they were sentenced to be beheaded, which was carried into execution on Tower Hill.

Arnheim did not remain in London to witness the execution of his confederates, whose lives had purchased his liberty ; but returned to the continent, where he ultimately entered into the service of the King of France, that monarch being the highest bidder he could find for his services.

THE END

LONDON : Printed and Published by E. Lloyd, 12, Salisbury Square, Fleet Street.

www.ingramcontent.com/pod-product-compliance
Lightning Source LLC
Chambersburg PA
CBHW081157170626
46813CB00009B/3223